DOWN IN FLAMES

SILVER TONGUED DEVILS BOOK 1

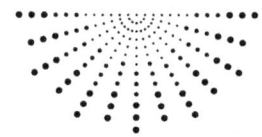

SAMANTHA CONLEY

DOWN
in Flames

SAMANTHA CONLEY

Cover Design – Amanda Walker PA and Design Services

Editing –Dana Hook of Rebel Edit and Design

❀ Created with Vellum

For my Granny,
You always told me I could do whatever I wanted, be whatever I
wanted. I love and miss you, everyday

DOWN IN FLAMES

SILVER TONGUED DEVILS

One night. One mistake. A relationship down in flames.

Kristen Daniels has worked for years to achieve her dreams. But that one night changes everything, shattering her perfect life.

Brett Ingles is on top of the world. His band is finally topping the charts and playing sold-out shows. He has a beautiful fiancé he loves with all his heart. One mistake could ruin it all.

Derek Calloway has always been someone his friends could depend on. He never intended to fall in love with her. She's off limits and he knows it. But the heart wants what the heart wants. He just hopes she's worth the risk.

PROLOGUE

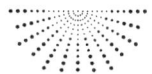

Kristen

"Damn, this place is packed," I mutter as we pull into the parking lot of Jake's Bar. I pull my POS Nissan into the closest available spot, next to a jacked-up truck around the back. "Mal, it's going to be hell for you, walking that far to the door in those shoes," I chuckle. My friend, Mallory, loves her high heels; the higher the better. I guess if I was barely breaking five feet tall, I'd need the boost too. I look in the rearview mirror to see her stick her tongue out at me. I grin back.

"We can't all be tall like you and Camryn, you know," she snaps back. "All right, bitches, let's party!" she yells as she opens the back door. Me and Camryn follow her out and we head for the entrance at the front. Mallory takes the lead, moving carefully across the lot in her hooker heels. I must admit, she looks hot in her short black skirt and red halter top, which shows off her lithe form. Not to mention, her long black hair and perky boobs. Sometimes I think I hate her a little bit for how much she eats, yet stays so damn skinny.

"Ten bucks says she falls," Camryn whispers.

"That's not very nice," I whisper back. Camryn isn't being mean, just observant. "I just hope she doesn't twist her ankle or something," I mutter. I don't wear heels, being more of a flats or sneakers kind of girl. At five-nine, I don't need the extra height. It's already hard enough to find a guy taller than me as it is.

After navigating the gravel strewn parking lot, we get to the door and walk inside. And man, is it loud. The band that's playing is rocking out. I immediately start moving to the beat, swaying my hips as the bass vibrates through my body. I holler to Camryn that I'm going to try and find us a table while they go get drinks at the bar. I'm the DD for the night, which is fine, since I don't drink a whole lot.

I spot an empty bar top and move to snag it. Weaving my way through the crowded dance floor, trying not to run in to anyone, I go to sidestep some guy, when he grabs my hips and tries to wrap himself around me. The alcohol fumes coming off of him could choke a horse. I try to pry him off, but he's not letting go. We're right in front of the stage, and I can't see security anywhere. The dude isn't budging, and he's getting really handsy at this point.

Suddenly, someone steps up to us and grabs the guy around the neck, putting him in a choke hold. Mr. Handsy lets go of me and I stumble back a bit, bumping in to someone else. That's as far as I can go since we've gathered quite an audience. Even the band has stopped playing. I glance at the stage and realize the guy who saved me is the singer of the band. I hear one of the band members call for a guy and a mountain of a man with 'Security' on his shirt moves toward us. I look back at my savior and holy moly, he's freaking hot—and tall. It's not often I have to crane my neck to look at a guy's face. Out of the corner of my eye, I see security grab Mr. Handsy, but I can't quit looking at the guy in front of me.

"Are you okay?" he asks me. I can only nod my head. "Were you headed to that table over there?" He points to the empty table. I nod again, and he leads me over to the table with his hand on my back. It feels like a furnace there, like I don't have a shirt between his hand and my skin. "I'm Brett, by the way."

"Kristen," I reply.

"Okay then, Kristen. Enjoy the rest of the show and I'll catch you later." He winks at me, then heads back to the stage and the band kicks back up.

Somehow, the girls find the table and gather around with drinks in hand. Camryn hands me a bottle of water. "What the hell happened? We saw the singer jump off the stage and into the crowd, then the security guy was moving that way."

"Some guy decided he needed to molest me, and the singer saved me," I inform her.

I can't stop looking at Brett. I swear he keeps looking over at me too. He looks so amazingly sexy with his dark spiky hair and dark eyes. Killer smile. He's wearing a black T-shirt that looks too small, showing off his toned body. Tattoos of some sort run down both arms, and his voice is like a shot of whiskey, smooth and strong. He's up there belting out lyrics and moving around the stage. I check my chin for drool, because DAMN! I swear every time he looks in my direction, he looks directly at me. But that's crazy, right?

As the night goes on, I watch as the same waitress brings the band bottles of water and beer in-between songs. Brett always says something to her, which makes me jealous. But, after she walks away, he looks over at me and smiles, making my heart pound hard against my chest.

"Kris!" Camryn snaps her fingers in front of my face to get my attention. "That guy has only had eyes for you tonight. You might be getting lucky, and it's about damn time, girl!" My face blushes scarlet at her words. So, it's been a bit of a dry spell for me, but it's been a busy four years in nursing school. That's the reason we came out tonight, to celebrate finishing our finals. We're going to graduate with our Bachelor of Science in Nursing degrees. It's been a long, hard road. Between classes, studying, and working, I had no time to date. And I'm not a one-night stand kind of girl.

The waitress appears at our table with fresh drinks. "These are from the band," she says, giving me a sly smile. "I brought you a strawberry vodka lemonade, hold the vodka. I figured since you're drinking water, you're the designated driver for the night." She places the drinks on the table in front of each of us, making sure the virgin one with the straw is in front of me. "Brett asked that you stick around for a while. They're almost done for the night." She looks me over curiously and says, "He never asks for a particular girl to stick around. They usually do that on their own. My cousin must see something he likes." She gives me a quick smile and disappears into the crowd, and I'm left speechless.

Just then, Brett steps up to the mic and starts to speak, pulling my attention back to the stage.

"Thank you, ladies and gentlemen, for coming out tonight. I hope y'all had a fuckin' blast because we sure as hell did. For all you who don't know us, let me make some introductions. On my left here is Isaac, our lead guitarist." Isaac does a quick wave and flashes a devastating grin, then plays some sick rifts on his guitar. Some of the girls in the place scream. "We got Jason on the drums." Jason pounds out a heavy beat. His arms move so fast, they're a blur. "On my right is my best friend and bassist, Derek." Derek waves and plays a deep beat. "I'm Brett, and we're The Silver Tongued Devils. Thanks for being such an amazing audience tonight."

The band keeps playing for an hour more, and we're having a blast. I know most of the songs they cover since they're not a country band. These guys rock hard, and I'm having the time of my life. I'm sure it has more to do with the sexy singer up on stage and him wanting me to hang around.

"Thanks again, everyone, and we'll catch y'all next time!"

The band retreats from the stage and some of the house lights come on, just as some rock music starts to play on the sound system. I look at my girls, and they're both drunk as skunks. I look at my watch and wonder how long it will be before Brett comes out, or if he forgot. Just as the thought crosses my mind, a warm hand lands on my shoulder, and I swear I feel a shock go through me.

"I'm glad you waited," he breathes in my ear. God, so am I. I turn to look at him and my breath catches in my throat. I have to take a second so I don't come off looking like an idiot. All the other band members come over to the table. Derek brings a girl with him, saving me from saying something stupid. Brett introduces the band to us again, and I introduce the girls.

"So, what brings y'all out tonight?" Brett asks. Mallory— poor drunken Mallory—slurs out, "We just finished school." Brett looks at me and I shrug.

"We just finished our finals for class, and we're officially done. Now we wait for our official grades to come out and the

5

ink to dry on our diplomas. So, we decided to come out and celebrate. We don't get out that much. Well, some of us don't."

"Where did y'all go to school? Somewhere local?" Brett inquires.

"TWU," I reply. He raises his eyebrow in question. "Texas Woman's University. We just finished with the nursing program."

"Wow, congratulations. Let me buy you girls another round of drinks to celebrate." He waves his hand at the waitress who delivered our drinks earlier, and I watch as she loads up her tray. She brings the drinks over, and even remembers to bring me a virgin one. Is it sad I think it's sexy, the way he holds his beer bottle? The way his throat moves when he swallows? I want to lick that stray drop of beer from his bottom lip. He catches me staring and gives me a smile. My cheeks heat as my blush rises.

We spend the rest of the night drinking and talking, with Brett and I in our own little world. This is definitely one of the best nights of my life.

Brett

I SEE THIS TALL, blonde, built girl walking through the crowd, wearing tight jeans with a slouchy sapphire blue shirt that hangs off one shoulder. She's weaving her way through the sea of people, heading toward the right side of the stage, when a guy we've been having trouble with all night grabs her by the hips and gives her his best anaconda impression. I look over to signal Tom in the back, but he's talking to someone, not seeing what is happening down in front. I jump off the stage and grab the guy to pull him off her. The band stops playing and Isaac hollers for Tom to get to the stage. I keep a firm grip on the guy until Tom arrives and escorts him out. I've had enough of him for the night. He should've been cut off earlier.

I escort the blonde to the empty table a few rows from the stage, ask her name, and head back to the stage so we can finish up our set. During one of our breaks, Melissa brings the band some water. I lean down to take them from her. "Lis, you see the blonde in the blue shirt over there on the right? Sitting with the two other girls?" She nods. "Would you send them a round of drinks from us? And ask the blonde to stick around after our set."

Melissa gives me a look, and I know what it means. I never lack for female attention, so it's unusual for me to ask about a girl. I glance over at her and smile before turning back to the guys to finish our set.

I keep glancing in her direction, and every time our eyes meet, I give her a little smile. I force myself to look away from her, but it's damn hard. She draws me like a moth to a flame. After introducing the guys, I give them a little solo time. We play for about another hour, then thank everyone for coming out.

Once we're backstage, I grab a towel and wipe off my face. "There's a beautiful woman out there waiting for me to come back out, and she has friends," I tell the guys.

Jason doesn't look impressed, but he's not one to make a show about the ladies. I can't remember the last time I saw him with one. Isaac, the player, grins. I know Derek could care less, since he has a girlfriend who's already out there waiting for

7

him. I grab a clean shirt out of my bag, change, and head back out to the bar.

I breathe a sigh of relief when I see she stayed. I reintroduce the guys, in case they didn't catch it during the show, and Kristen introduces her friends to us. I can tell the little dark-haired girl is a goner. As small as she is, it probably doesn't take a lot of alcohol to get her drunk. When she slurs out the answer to a question, she nearly slides off her stool. Jason is the one to steady her, keeping a hand on her back to hold her steady. Huh, interesting. Isaac, being Isaac, has moved toward the redhead in the group.

Kristen and I sit and talk for a couple hours, until my uncle starts turning off the lights. I can't remember a time a girl has kept my attention without sex being involved, but she's beautiful, smart, and captivating. How did I get so lucky? This may be the best night of my life.

CHAPTER ONE

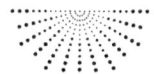

Kristen

Something startles me awake. Maybe the plane hit some turbulence. I never thought I would fall asleep on a plane, but I've been working my ass off lately to be able to get a four day weekend to fly up to Minneapolis to see Brett and the guys. I haven't seen Brett in six months, and Skype and texts just aren't cutting it anymore. I haven't even gotten to talk to him in the past four days, with the band on tour, and me working 12-hour shifts at the hospital. If I ever decide to work five straight, 12-hour days again, someone needs to shoot me for stupidity. At least I'm not stuck in economy class and have a little room in my seat to stretch out, all thanks to the band's manager, Brian. I'm glad that he's helping me surprise Brett. The only thing that sucks is that my flight was delayed due to mechanical difficulties, so we took off nearly two hours late. That means I won't get to see Brett before the concert, and I'll more than likely miss the concert altogether. I'd texted Brian about the delay, and he said he would have a car at the airport to pick me up to take me to the venue or the hotel the band is staying at. We'll actually get to stay in Minneapolis for three days before the band has to leave for the next leg of their tour.

I sit here and think back to the beginning, when I met Brett and the guys for the first time. Brett and I dating, spending as much time together as we could between our schedules. I was always working at the hospital, while he worked construction for Derek's uncle at Calloway Construction. But I wouldn't trade it for the world. It's been a roller coaster five years. It all fell into place when Brian Jefferies walked into the bar one weekend. Brian had only listened to the band play a couple of songs before he decided he wanted to represent them. Brian got them on satellite radio, and they became the hottest thing on the radio overnight. They started playing at different bars, opening for other bands, and gathered a huge following. Now they were on their second headlining tour with the release of their second album. Brian had them traveling all over the place promoting the new album. After Minneapolis, the guys are heading to Europe for the last leg of the tour. Man, I wish I could go with them, but with work and school, there's no way. Maybe after I finish my current semester I could fly over for a week or two. Lord knows I have enough vacation time.

Sometimes, I wonder what the hell I was thinking, going back to school for my master's degree, but a girl's gotta do what a girl's gotta do. My dream is to be a pediatric nurse practitioner. I love working with kids, and I love my job at the children's hospital.

I glance down and stare at the big rock sitting on my left ring finger, as the glow of the overhead light makes it sparkle. Brett proposed to me at Jake's Bar before this tour started four months ago. I'm just so excited, thinking about our future together. I can't wait to see him tonight.

I'm pulled from my thoughts as the pilot announces our landing, so I gather my stuff and get ready to get off this tin can. I'm glad I only packed my carry-on, so I won't have to wait at the baggage claim. I shoot off a quick text to Brian to let him know I landed, and he suggests I go to the hotel and wait for Brett. He's given the driver the key to the room, which is great for me. It'll give me time to freshen up before Brett arrives.

I don't have to wait long before the driver pulls up and whisks me away to the hotel. Pulling up, I feel out of place. I dress for comfort when I fly, so I'm in a T-shirt, jeans, and flip-flops. I can see the doorman giving me a weird look as I get the key from the driver and he gives my carry-on to the bellhop that comes to the car, then off we go to the elevator. We get to the room and the bellhop puts my bag inside the door as I look around the room. Holy moly, this place is nice. Way too rich for my blood. The bellhop clears his throat and I realize he's waiting for a tip. I dig in my pocket, but only pull out a couple of ones. "I'm so sorry," I tell him. "It's all the cash I have on me."

"Thank you," he says formally and leaves the room.

Great. He probably thinks I'm cheap, but I never carry cash. Maybe I need to start.

Brian texts me to let me know that Brett should be at the hotel within the hour. I head to the bathroom to freshen up and change clothes. I brought one of the slinky dresses that Brett likes to surprise him, then I sit and wait.

I'm sitting in the chair when I hear someone outside the door, so I turn off the TV, ready to surprise him. I can hear him say something, then a female giggles. I pause. Maybe it's not him. I mean, why would there be a girl with him? I hear fumbling with the door, like the key won't work, but finally, the door opens and Brett walks in with his lips attached to some barely dressed blonde. Following them through the door is an even less dressed brunette with her hands all over his ass. I can hear her talking about all the things she wants to do to him. I'm completely frozen from shock.

The brunette starts to pull his shirt off and he only detaches his lips from the blonde so the shirt can go over his head. He looks at the brunette and says, "Strip and get on the bed." She eagerly complies. He turns back to the blonde and says, "Take my dick out and suck it like a good girl." The blonde can't get her hands on his belt fast enough. How long am I going to sit here and watch this? They're so caught up in what they're doing, they don't even see me. I feel like I'm in a nightmare. I watch as the blonde takes his dick into her mouth. Brett groans and sways on his feet. He just keeps staring at the ceiling and moaning. I glance at the brunette and she's buck naked with one hand on her tit and one on her pussy. Brett pulls the blonde off his dick and tells her to get on the bed too.

"Daddy," the brunette moans. "I've got some more blow for us. I want you to snort it off my pussy." She has a dreamy look on her face and it dawns on me that they're all high as kites.

I can't watch anymore. I spy my carry-on by the door, so I stand and make my way toward it. As I open the door, I hear one of the girls ask "Who's that?" I glance back to see Brett look at me—look through me.

"That's nobody," he says.

Nobody. My heart shatters into a million pieces. I never knew my heart could hurt so badly.

I think I'm in shock. I don't even notice my surroundings. I head out the door and quickly throw on some clothes from my bag in the hallway. Once I'm dressed, I take the elevator down and make my way through the lobby to the sidewalk. The doorman asks if I need anything.

"A cab," I say, and he waves one down.

"Where to, Miss?"

"The airport."

I feel like I'm moving in slow motion and I can't think. Before I know it, I'm at the airport. Thank God I can use my debit card to pay for the cab fare. I move to the ticket agent, and I'm so out of it, I don't even hear her speaking to me, not until she reaches over the counter and touches my shoulder.

"Oh, I'm sorry. I need to get back to Dallas as soon as possible." I know she can see that something's wrong and takes pity on me. I hand her my ticket and she starts working on her computer. Luckily, there's a flight leaving in an hour and they have a few open seats in economy. I take it and head to the gate.

Finally, I'm on the plane and headed home. But what is home anymore?

CHAPTER TWO

Brett

I wake up with my head pounding and my mouth tasting like ass. I blink a few times, trying to clear my vision. I stretch my arms out and hit something solid and warm. What the fuck? I look to my left and see blonde hair sticking out from under the covers. I smile, wondering when Kris got here, but I realize I'm in Minneapolis and she's back home. Fuck! What the fuck did I do? I try to inch away from the blonde and get off the bed when I run into another warm body. I glance over my shoulder and see a brunette smiling at me. I can't tell if she's pretty or not. Her makeup is smeared all over her face, like she's been rode hard and put away wet. Jesus Christ, what the fuck happened?

"Morning, Daddy," she says to me. "Ready for another round? We don't have to wake her up. It can just be us this time. I didn't get enough last night." She licks her lips and eyes me up and down.

I just look at her. I have to get them out of here. Jesus, what am I going to do? I start moving to the end of the bed and find I'm naked, and so are they.

"You need to wake your friend up and get the fuck outta here," I tell her as I run my hands through my hair.

"Don't be that way, Daddy," she pouts. "We can still have some fun."

"I said get the fuck out! Now!" I yell at her, waking up the blonde. Damn, she looks worse than the brunette. "Get the fuck out before I call security and they take your asses out!"

I turn and walk into the bathroom and shut the door. I can hear them moving around, and I can only pray that they're getting dressed and getting the hell out. I take a piss and hear the door to the room slam shut. I double check to make sure they're gone before I jump in the shower. I hope it wakes me up because I can't remember a damn thing about last night, not even the concert. The hot water feels great as I soap up, making sure to wash my dick really, really good. Fuck, did we use protection? Last thing I need is to catch something and pass it on to Kris. Fuck, I love that girl to death. What the fuck was I doing with those sluts? I can't believe I cheated on her. Or did I? Shit, I think it's pretty obvious, as I woke up naked with two chicks in my bed.

I step out of the shower and grab a towel. I'm drying off when I notice a maroon T-shirt, a pair of jeans and flip-flops on the floor. I know they're not mine, and I doubt they belong to the sluts. I wrap the towel around my waist and bend down to pick the shirt up, and recognize it immediately. It's Kris's favorite TWU shirt. Lifting it up to my nose, I smell apples, like the lotion Kris wears all the time. I drop it to the floor. No, it can't be. She's in Dallas.

I hear my phone ring in the other room and hurry out to grab it, but it stops ringing before I get to it. I look around the room. The bed is in shambles. There's an empty liquor bottle and baggies littering the floor. What the hell? I grab one of the baggies, finding traces of white powder inside. Jesus Christ, I've really fucked up. I grab my phone. It's noon, and I've missed six calls— two from Derek and four from Brian. I call Brian back first.

He picks up on the first ring. "Hello? You finally awake, Sleeping Beauty? Have a busy night?" he chuckles. "Did you like your surprise? Is that why you can't answer the phone?"

Surprise? What surprise? I stiffen. "What surprise?" I ask, not sure if I even want to know.

"Kristen, you dumbass. I thought it would be a nice surprise for you two to get a little time together before we head off to Europe for a few months. I hate that she missed the show, but she said it was fine for her to go straight to the hotel and wait for you. She said she got there okay...Brett? Are you there?"

My mind is whirling. Kris was here? Last night? "Brian, I think..." I swallow hard. "I think I fucked up." I drop down onto the bed and put my head in my hand. I hear Brian say he'll be here in ten and hang up.

I call Derek. Maybe he can help. Help with what? I don't know yet.

"What's up, dickhead? I was trying to get some more shut-eye," he mumbles into the phone after the fourth ring.

"I need you, man. I fucked up, and it's really bad."

"Be there in a minute. Let me throw some clothes on. I'm a few doors down."

Derek hangs up, and I decide dressing is a good idea. I grab a pair of jeans out of my bag and slip them on, then turn around and stare at the bed. I can't believe this. Maybe Derek will have some answers. We've been friends since we were kids, going through everything together from football, baseball, high school, and the death of my parents from a car accident. Maybe he'll know what to do and get me out of this fucked-up situation.

When I hear the knock at the door, I open and let him in, giving him an opportunity to take in the room. "Damn. Did you have a party in here and not invite me?" he laughs. I just look at him, and the smile drops from his face. "What? Is this what you called me about?" he asks. I sit down on the bed.

"I fucked up, Derek, and I don't even remember it. I woke up, naked, with two chicks in bed with me." I can't even look at him. I put my elbows on my knees and my head in my hands. I think I'm going to be sick. He doesn't say anything, and after what seems like an eternity, I look at him to find him staring at me. "Say something, please?" I plead with him. His face grows hard.

"What the fuck were you thinking, Brett?" he yells at me, making my head throb. He starts pacing around the room. "You're telling me you cheated on Kris? I can't fucking believe you. She's the best fucking thing that's ever happened to you, and this is how you treat her?" He's looking at me like he doesn't even know me.

"I don't know, man. I can't even remember last night. I can barely remember the concert and going backstage, but everything after that is a blur. I don't know what I did." I take a deep breath. "I know I fucked up. I need to know what to do."

CHAPTER THREE

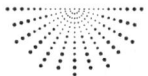

Derek

I look over at my best friend and can't believe what he's telling me. He cheated on Kristen. My mind is blown. He's looking at me like he hopes I have the answer for him, but I sure as hell don't. I'm still reeling from the words that came out of his mouth. I look around the room and take it in. I see the wrecked bed, the liquor bottles on the floor, and—what the hell? I bend over and pick up a little baggie off the floor.

"What the fuck is this?" I yell at him again. "You're doing drugs now? Do I even know you anymore?" Maybe that was a little drastic, but damn. One thing we always talked about was if we ever made it big, we wouldn't fall into the drugs that run rampant in the rock world. I turn to look at him, and he has this blank look on his face.

"I—I don't know," he stutters out. I spot a chair sitting off to the side and plop down into it.

"Okay, let's break this down. What's the last thing you

remember?" I ask him. The last time I remember seeing him was backstage. All of us had gone to the green room, but he showed up about fifteen minutes after everyone else did. I didn't get to say anything to him because the place was packed with people, and I was busy trying to get with a cute blonde. I vaguely remember him walking in with two girls, but I really wasn't paying that much attention. I was too focused on the blonde's tits that were threatening to pop out of her top. Brett is the only guy in the band with a steady girl, so the rest of us hook up with the groupies. I remember leaving with the girl and heading back to the hotel, and I didn't see Brett again until this morning.

"I remember leaving the stage and thinking it was a great show. I followed y'all to the green room and that's it. The rest is a blur. Just occasional flashes." As he's finishing his sentence, there's a knock on the door.

"That's probably Brian. I called him too, and he told me the most fucked-up part." I head to the door and let Brian in.

"Dude, what the hell's goin' on?" Brian asks.

"Saying Brett's had an interesting night is putting it mildly," I mumble back at him. Brian looks over my shoulder and spies Brett sitting on the bed.

He moves around me. "Brett? What's goin' on? Where's Kristen?"

Where's Kristen? She's here? Oh, fuck. Brett looks at me, then back to Brian.

"I don't know. I don't remember seeing her last night. All I know is I woke up with two naked chicks in the bed, and not remembering a damn thing about last night." I don't think I've ever seen Brett look the way he does at this moment, except for when we found out his parents had been killed.

"Start from the beginning," Brian says, and Brett tells the story as he remembers it. Brian looks around the room with a keen eye. "I see the bottles, but those sure as hell better not be drugs. You know what I don't see? Condom wrappers. Please tell me you wrapped your dick last night before you stuck it in who knows what."

Brian's right. I don't see any wrappers anywhere. I lift the covers off the bed and look underneath, then under the bed and around the floor. Not one single wrapper. Son of a bitch. I look over at Brett, and I swear he's turned green.

"Okay, first things first," I begin. "What does Kristen have to do with last night?" I look at Brian and Brett. Brett still looks a little too green, so I look back to Brian.

"She flew in last night to surprise Brett. Her plane left late and she didn't get here early enough to see him before the show. I had the driver drop her off here to wait for him. I know she made it here. I already verified it with the driver and the hotel staff."

Holy shit! This is a disaster of fucking epic proportions. "Where is she now?" Damn, if she was here, where the fuck is she now? Does she know what went down last night?

"She was here at some point," Brett says quietly. I look over at him. "When I got out of the shower, I found her clothes on the bathroom floor."

"How do you know they're hers?" I ask. He gets up, goes to the bathroom and returns with a maroon T-shirt and throws it at me. I catch it up close to my face and smell apples. Yep, it's Kristen's.

"So, the question is, where the fuck is she now?" Brett stares at the floor.

Brian looks up from texting on his phone. "I have my

assistant checking on some things. Hopefully, we'll have an answer soon. Have you tried calling her?" he asks Brett.

I can't believe we hadn't thought to call her, especially if Brett knew she was here last night. Brett doesn't make a move, so I grab my phone out of my pocket and scroll through my contacts, hitting her number. The call goes straight to voicemail, which is unusual. She never has her phone off in case her work calls. Now I'm worried if she's safe.

"Straight to voicemail," I tell the guys.

Brian looks up from his phone. "She flew back to Dallas last night."

Brett grabs his phone and dials. I can hear him chanting, "Pick up, pick up," but his call also goes voicemail. "Kris, baby, if you're there, pick up. Please. I'm worried." Then he hangs up the phone.

Almost instantly, it rings back. "Thank God," he mutters. "Kris, I...what? No, baby...Please, Kris—" He lowers the phone and looks down at the screen. "She says she's done. She's leaving." I see his eyes well up and a tear slides down his cheek.

Shit.

CHAPTER FOUR

Kristen

I feel like I'm walking around in a fog. I pull into the drive-way, and I can't even remember the drive home. I can only hope that I drove safely. I park in front of the door, not bothering to park in the garage. I unlock the front door and drop my bag on the floor. It sounds so loud in the empty house.

I head to the kitchen and open the fridge. Not a whole lot in there. I'd cleaned it out and hadn't had time to go grocery shop-ping. I need alcohol. I go to the cabinet and pull out a bottle of Jack Daniels and head to the living room. Plopping down on the couch, I grab the remote off the table and turn on the TV. It's some reality show that I've never seen or heard of, with a man and woman screaming at each other about the both of them cheating. So not what I need to hear right now. I scroll through the guide and find Ghostbusters on. I love this movie. I put down the remote and check the time. It's just a little after four am. I take the top off the whiskey and take a healthy swig, wincing when it burns my throat. I take another and another until the room starts to spin.

I set the bottle on the table and glance at the picture sitting there, the one of me and Brett right after he proposed. I see the glow on my face and the goofy smile. He's looking down at me like I'm the only person in the world. What utter bullshit. I wonder if he was doing this shit before he proposed. How long has this been going on? What the hell did I do wrong? I pick up the picture and trace his face with my finger, then I start to cry. Not just cry, but big, gut-wrenching sobs that shake my whole body. I cry until there are no more tears and I'm only occasionally gasping for air. I fall asleep on the couch with the picture clutched to my chest.

I WAKE UP WITH A START. I hear the back door open, then someone moving around in the kitchen. I get up to find Nelda, our housekeeper, getting out some cleaning supplies from under the sink.

"Hey, Nelda," I say. She jumps and turns around with her hand over her heart.

"Jesus, you scared me to death. I thought you were going to be gone until Monday?" She looks at me strangely, and I can only imagine what I look like after my crying jag.

"Nelda, is there any way you could come back tomorrow? I'm not feeling good right now, and I'm in a pretty shitty mood. I don't want to take the chance of taking it out on you."

She looks at me with pity in her eyes and says she'll come back tomorrow after church, and that she hopes I feel better.

Not frigging likely, and not any time soon. Nelda lets herself out the back door and I head back to the living room. I sit down on the couch and notice it's just a little after eight. What the hell am I going do? Do I confront him? Let him explain? That's stupid. I mean, what the hell is there to explain? He cheated on me, and not with one, but two women at the same time.

I head up the stairs to our bedroom. Once inside, I stare at the king size bed we share, with its soft sheets and warm comforter. We compromised on the heavy comforter since I have to have it cold when I sleep, with the fan blowing on me. Brett always says I'm trying to freeze him out so he'll cuddle up to me at night. I sit on my side and remember the last night we were in here together.

I'm in the bathroom getting ready for bed. I grab my hair to braid it and snag my ring. I glance down at my left hand and smile when the diamonds catch the light. I can't believe he proposed tonight. I look in the mirror and see the silly little smile I have on my face. I quickly change out of my skinny jeans and blouse and put on my tank top and boy shorts. I made sure to grab the ones that Brett really likes, the ones where the bottom half of my ass shows. I grab my apple-scented lotion and lather it on my arms and legs. I told Brett once that I had thought about getting a more grown-up scented lotion, but he said that he loves it, and every time he sees an apple or smells that scent, he thinks of me. He's so sweet.

I open the bathroom door and see him lying on the bed. He's stripped down to his boxer briefs, and looks at me as I come out. I stop and stare just outside the door. Damn, he's sexy. I skim my eyes over him, starting from his messy brown hair to his dark brown eyes, then his full soft lips and strong jawline.

He moves a little and it makes his pecs flex and his abs contract. I love to lick my way down his six pack, all the way to that sexy as hell V. I notice the twitch in his briefs as he starts to get hard. That makes me a lucky lady. He's hung, and he knows how to use it. I continue down his muscular thighs and strong calves. Is it sad that I even find his feet sexy?

"You just gonna stand there, or get the hell over here where you belong?" he asks with a little smile.

I walk over to him, putting a little extra sway in my hips. I feel silly, but his eyes are eating me up. I reach his side of the bed and he grabs me by the hips and pulls me over him until I'm straddling his stomach.

"You're so beautiful," he says as he looks me over. I never really believe it, but when he looks at me this way, I can. He runs his hands up my thighs to my ass and squeezes. His hands can cover my whole ass. "Damn, I love when you wear these." He keeps his left hand on my ass and moves his right over my rib cage, between my breasts, then around the back of my neck. He gently pulls me down on his chest.

"I love you so fucking much, Kris," he says and he presses his lips to mine. I smile against his lips.

"I love you too." He pulls me in for a harder kiss and slips his tongue between my lips. I open up and let him in. My tongue plays with his and our kiss becomes more passionate, like we can't get enough of each other. He moves his hand from around my neck, down to my breast and squeezes. He grips my nipple with his finger and thumb and twists it a little. It feels so damn good. He moves his hands to the bottom of my tank top and slowly pushes it up my torso. We break the kiss long enough to pull it off, then I move back to his mouth. He takes his hands and puts them back on my ass, then slips his finger underneath the lace, close to my core. One finger skims over my lips. I should be embarrassed with how wet I am, but he moans his approval against my mouth. Before I even realize it, he has us rolled over in the middle of the bed and is pressing me into the mattress. He moves his mouth down my jaw to my neck. He nips me on the side and I flinch a little. He knows that will turn me on quicker than anything. He moves down my neck and zeroes in on my left nipple. He licks around it, then nips the tip with his teeth. I never realized I liked a little pain with my pleasure until Brett. His other hand gives my right breast a squeeze and continues on its downward path. He pulls back a little to allow his hand to slide in the front of my panties. Dipping his finger into my wetness, he moves his fingers to my clit. He rubs it slowly, and my body jerks.

"Like that, baby?" I can only nod. He sits up and begins to pull my panties down. Once he pulls them past me feet, he puts my leg on his shoulder and bends down. He slowly licks up my center, and zeroes in on my clit like a missile. He licks and flicks his tongue until I'm crying out. He pushes two thick fingers into my core and I fly. My orgasm is still ripping through me when he hooks my legs with his arms and slams his thick cock into me. He stretches me nearly to the point of pain. He pulls out slowly and thrusts back in, hard, just how I like it.

"Fuck, you feel so good, babe. Look at that pretty pussy take my cock." He knows that talking dirty does it for me too. And boy, does it. He keeps thrusting and retreating while he picks up the pace. I can feel myself building again.

"You gonna come on my cock, babe? I want you to suck me in and squeeze me hard." He moves his hand, dips it in our wetness and puts two fingers on my clit and rubs. That's all it takes, and I explode. There's no other word for it. I can feel myself clenching around him and the world starts to grow black. I can feel him thrust a few more times before he stiffens. "Fuck, yes, baby. So fucking good." He puts his weight on me and kisses me softly on the lips.

"I love you, babe. You're the best thing that's ever happened to me. I don't know what I did to deserve having you in my life, but I thank God that you decided to go to Jake's that night to celebrate." He moves to my side and cuddles me to him.

"Me too, Brett. Me too."

I shake myself out of the memory. I don't think anything is going to make me forget what I saw last night. I can't stay here. I can't sleep in this bed, knowing what happened. I move to the closet and pull out my suitcase, place it on the bed and open it up. I go back to the closet and start grabbing clothes. Not the ones that he's bought me, but the ones I've bought. I want nothing from him. I clean out my drawers in the dresser and move to the bathroom. As I walk in, I hear the phone ring. I don't want to answer, but I stand still. It goes to the machine. "Kris, baby, if you're there, pick up. Please. I'm worried." The nerve of him.

I'm just going to ignore him, but then I find myself grabbing the phone and hitting redial. "Kris—" is all I let him get out before I start crying.

"I can't do this, Brett. Not after last night. I won't be your 'nobody.' I'm leaving." I hang up the phone and move to the bathroom. With tears streaming down my face, I gather up my makeup and hair stuff and walk back to shove it all in the suitcase. I take off my ring and place it on the table on his side of the bed. When I reach the bottom of the stairs, I remember that Nelda is supposed to come back. I write her a quick note, letting her know that I'll be gone for a while and she won't have to come as often, maybe every other week to dust since no one will be here until Brett returns home. She always keeps a couple meals in the freezer in case they're needed. I know that Brett has her salary deposited into her bank account. I grab my phone and call Mallory. "Mal, I need a favor. Can I stay with you for a couple days?"

CHAPTER FIVE

Brett

I can't believe what's happening. I thought when she called me back I could try to explain, try to make her understand... make her understand what? That I did the unthinkable? That I broke her heart? Just hearing her crying on the phone and the desolation in her voice makes me sick to my stomach. How could I ever hurt her that way?

"Brian, I have to get home. I have to see her. I have to make her understand it was a mistake."

"I'm already working on it, kid. There's a flight out in two hours and you're on it. You have to be ready to fly out Monday to Europe, though, no matter what. The rest of us depend on you." He messes around on his phone and I hear my notification go off.

"There's your flight information. Good luck, Brett. You're going to need it. And we'll be having a discussion about this." He holds up one of the little baggies from the floor. "I'll get this cleaned up before housekeeping comes up. I don't want the press getting any of this mess; that's the last thing we need." Brian walks out the door and it shuts loudly behind him.

I look over at Derek, and he's still sitting in the chair on the other side of the room. "Could you grab my stuff out of the closet? I'll grab the stuff in the bathroom."

He nods his head and stiffly moves to the closet and grabs the suitcase. I grab the little bag in the bathroom and shove everything into it, not caring how it falls in. I move quickly out of the bathroom and see that Derek has only laid the suitcase on the bed.

"Dude, come on. I have to hurry to catch that flight."

"How could you do this? I don't understand how you could hurt her this way." He looks at and walks out the door.

What the hell? Shouldn't he be on my side? I know that he and Kristen have become close friends over the years, but he's my best friend. Shouldn't he be helping me figure this out and working to help me get her back? Hell, I'll figure that out later. Right now, I have to get to the airport and get back to my girl and fix this.

I throw all the clothes I can in the suitcase. I hurry down to the elevator and only have to wait a minute before it arrives. I scare the poor lady already on the elevator as I practically throw my suitcase in. "Sorry," I mumble and hit the first floor button. I forget my manners, about letting a lady go first, and rush off the elevator when we hit the lobby. Once I'm out the front door, I see a car waiting outside. He opens the car door for me and grabs my suitcase, but he's moving slower than molasses. He finally gets in the driver's seat and looks at me in the rearview mirror.

"Do you need anything else, sir, before we leave?" I shake my head no.

"Nothing but your lead foot on the gas." He gives a quick smile, and with a little more oomph than I expected, we pull out into traffic. He must have taken me very seriously. He's driving like we're in a street race, but he gets me to the airport in record time, and to the right gate as well. I pull out my wallet while he's getting my suitcase and hand him a hundred dollar bill.

"Thanks, man." I grab my suitcase and haul ass into the airport.

I've got my bag checked and I'm sitting in first class, but I can't enjoy it. All I can think about is how Kris sounded on the phone and how I'm the cause. We land fifteen minutes ahead of schedule, and I thank Brian for having a driver waiting here for me too. I grab my suitcase as soon as it hits the carousel and hurry out the door. I find the driver quickly, load up, and we're on the road.

WHEN WE PULL up in front of the house, I throw some cash in the front seat for a tip and jump out. "Just put the bag by the door!" I yell back over my shoulder. I reach the door and try to open it, but it's locked. I start feeling around my pockets for my keys and fumble with the lock to get the door open.

"Kris! Where are you?" I look in the living room. Not there. I see a bottle of Jack sitting on the table next to the remote and a picture frame. I glance in the kitchen, then head to the staircase, taking them two at a time while calling her name. But there's no answer. I fly through the door of our bedroom and stop dead in my tracks. The closet door is standing wide open and the dresser drawers are only partially closed. I put my hands on my head and spin around. No, no, no. This can't be happening.

I spy something out of the corner of my eye. I walk to my nightstand and find the engagement ring I bought just lying there. I pick it up. "Kris, baby, no," I whisper. "I need you too much." I turn to sit down on the side of the bed, but end up sliding down beside it. I just stare at the ring as I cry.

CHAPTER SIX

Derek

I walk out of the hotel room without even looking back at Brett. I still can't wrap my head around what the hell he did. Kris is the best fucking thing that's ever happened to him. Hell, I've become pretty attached to her myself. She's been in my life for five years, as well as his. She's been there for us all. When we were first starting out, she came to every show she could, sold our CDs, T-shirts, and even pimped us out on social media. She was even my shoulder to lean on when Stephanie and I called it quits. I'd always thought of her as one of the guys.

Until one day it changed, and I found myself in love with her. Not that I would ever act on what I felt for her; I respected Brett and her too much. They are so in love and I would never, ever try to mess with that. So, I tucked my feelings down deep and wished them the best. I really tied one on the night Brett proposed to her, though. I've always known that my feelings would have to stay hidden from them, but it still felt like I'd been stabbed in the heart.

It's no wonder every girl I take to bed resembles Kristen, but they'll never be her. I get my phone out of my pocket and call Kris. Straight to voicemail again.

"Kris, call me, please. I'm worried. What the hell happened last night?" Like I don't know. "Brian said you flew up here but no one's seen ya. Just let me know you're all right. I need to know that someone didn't snatch you off the street. Talk to me, girl."

I hang up and go into my hotel room. I see the mess in the room, but the girl from last night is gone. I guess she got tired of waiting since I hightailed it out this morning to go to Brett. I grab the empty bottle and the condom wrappers off the floor and throw them in the trash can. At least I was smart enough to wrap my dick.

I sit down on the side of the bed. What to do? We'll be in Minneapolis until Monday, then we fly out to London. We're all supposed to go bar hopping tonight to blow off some steam. We haven't really had a night to just relax. We're usually finishing a concert, then on the bus until the next stop. Damn, it was nice to sleep in a real bed last night. I lay back on the messy covers and grab a pillow for my head. Closing my eyes, I think back.

I walk up to the house and ring the bell. Brett hadn't answered his phone when I called, but I really need to talk to him or Kris. Nelda answers the door and lets me in. "Brett's not home, but Kristen is out back, swimming."

"Thanks, Nelda." I give her a quick kiss on the cheek and walk through the kitchen to the back patio door. I walk over to the side of the pool and sit on the end of one of the lounge chairs and stare off into space.

"Derek!" I look down to see Kris leaning on the edge of the pool. "I didn't know you were coming over. Brett went to go help Jake out for a little while. Did he forget you were coming?"

I take a deep breath. My chest still hurts. "No, it wasn't planned. I tried calling him but he didn't answer. I just needed to talk to him, or you. I found out Steph has been cheating on me."

Kris looks stunned. "What the hell? How? When?"

I think back to what I walked in on. I found the girl I'd spent the last two years with on her hands and knees, getting fucked from behind by some muscle-bound meathead looking guy on my bed. When she looked over at me standing in the doorway, she smiled. I just turned around and walked out.

I guess I expected her to follow me out, try to explain or something, but they continued to go at it. I got in my truck and started it up, but I just sat there, waiting to see if one of them would come out of the apartment door. It took half an hour before meathead walked out. I watched him walk to an ugly ass yellow car and get in. It dawned on me that I'd seen that car a few times in the parking lot.

That's when my phone rang. It was her. "'Lo?"

"Derek, where'd you run off to? I wanted to surprise you, thinking you'd join us. That's why we waited for you to come home." What the hell?

"You thought I would want to join in? What the fuck ever gave you that idea? I don't share. That's not even on my fantasy list. All I know is that I want your cheating ass out by the time I get back!"

"Babe, come on—"

"Just get out, Steph. I'm done with your ass." I put the truck in reverse and eased out of the spot, then pulled out into traffic.

A couple hours after driving around, I found myself at Brett's house.

"I walked in to find her fucking some guy in our bed."

"That fucking bitch," Kris hisses. "What the fuck was she thinking?"

"She was thinking I'd want to join them," I reply back.

"Well, she's an idiot. I can't stand a cheater. It's a hard limit for me. There's no building back any sort of trust after that."

I watch as Kris moves to the end of the pool and gets out. I can't help but notice her; she's got a great fucking body. Brett sure is a lucky fucker. She's dripping wet and wears a cute bikini. She doesn't have to wear one of those skimpy, show-all to the world kind of bikinis. She actually wears one made for swimming. She leans her head back and wrings out her long, wet hair. Her normal blonde looks brown. When she leans back, it thrusts her chest out and I can see her hard little nipples jutting through the material.

"Can you hand me that towel?" She shakes me out of my state. I look around and see the towel on the arm of the chair next to me, so I pick it up and walk it over to her. "Thanks." She bends over and I can only stare at the side of her plump, firm ass and long legs. She's not purposely doing it, but she's turning me on. Holy shit. Look away! This is Brett's girl. Your best friend's girl. Your ride or die friend's girl. I reassure myself that it's just a normal reaction to seeing a beautiful woman. "If you want, there are some drinks in the cooler." I walk over to the cooler and grab a bottle of beer.

"You want anything?"

"A bottle of water, please." I reach back in and grab a bottle from the bottom. The ice-cold water takes care of the problem that popped up earlier. I turn around to hand it to her and see that she has the towel wrapped around her. Thank God.

"You wanna stay for dinner? Nelda's making her famous enchiladas, and I think I'm in the mood for some margaritas."

She looks at me and I shrug. "Sounds good to me. How can I say no to Nelda's enchiladas?"

We walk back into the kitchen, and the smell of enchiladas fills the air. Nelda is at the stove stirring a pot, and I can only hope it's her Mexican rice. That shit is awesome. Nearly as good as the enchiladas. Kris mutters something about going upstairs to change and heads out of the kitchen.

"Food's almost ready. Brett called and said he's going to be later than he thought." I see Kris walk back in and she's on her phone, typing something back. I assume that Brett has texted her to let her know.

"Sounds great, Nelda. Kris said you were making enchiladas. Y'all couldn't get rid of me if you wanted to. Since you're only here once a week, maybe I can steal you for a day. Keep me knee-deep in enchiladas." She gives me a playful swat on the arm as she blushes. I move to the cabinets and grab some plates, while Kris reaches for some silverware. We place our stuff on the table and our hands touch. I swear a shock passes between us. Kris doesn't even react, so I guess it's all in my head.

"I'll grab the blender if you grab the stuff for margaritas." I don't know what she puts in her margaritas—she keeps it a secret—but they are the best I've ever had. I get the blender off the shelf in the pantry and sit it on the island. Kris walks back over with tequila and a bottle of yellow-green liquid, her secret mix.

"Get the ice, will ya?" she asks as she starts to pour stuff in the blender. I get the ice tub out of the freezer and hand it to her. She starts to whip up the drinks, and I head over to help Nelda get the enchiladas and rice on the table. Nelda says goodbye and heads out the door, toward the garage.

"Dish those bad boys up, Derek. I'm starving!" I make us both plates and sit down. She brings over two monster glasses of margaritas and we tuck in. Damn, the enchiladas are amazing. We eat and drink until we're stuffed. She refills our glasses and we head into the living room. I sit in a recliner and she sprawls out on the couch.

"Anything you wanna watch?" she asks and grabs the remote. I shake my head no and take another drink. She turns on the TV and one of my favorite movies is on.

"I love this movie," she gushes. We watch and laugh and drink a couple more pitchers of margaritas, and by the time Brett rolls in, we're both lit.

It's hard to believe that was two years ago. I ended up staying the night that night and got to repeat what had happened with Steph to Brett the next morning as I nursed a good hangover. I ended up staying with them for the next couple weeks while I dealt with Stephanie and her refusing to move out of the apartment. I'd forgotten that I added her to the lease a few months prior, so I moved out because I didn't want to deal with the drama. I finally got myself off our joint lease and found another apartment in another complex far, far away from Stephanie and her bullshit.

While I stayed with Brett and Kris, I saw the kind of relationship I wanted. They supported each other, and it was obvious how much they loved each other. And they expressed that love loudly. Sometimes, several times a night. I learned to sleep with headphones on. I felt sorry for any kids they had in the future.

But now that future may be in question with the way Brett fucked up. She had told me before that she couldn't stand a cheater, that it was a hard limit for her. Did Brett have a chance? And did I really want him to? As soon as that thought popped in my head, I felt horrible. But you can't help how you feel, right?

CHAPTER SEVEN

Kristen

I end up staying at Mallory's apartment. Thank goodness she has a spare bedroom that I can crash in and cry in peace. The only time she comes in is to replenish my junk food supply. I think I've lived on potato chips and chocolate ice cream. I've eaten, slept, and cried. I've watched weepy chick flicks and cried some more. She's a saint for putting up with me. I've kept my phone turned off for the most part, because every time I turn it back on, I have tons of voicemails and texts. I finally texted Brett back to let him know that I was okay, but I didn't want to talk to him. The betrayal hurts too much. I decide to call Derek back. He's the only other person I can talk to. I dial his number and he answers on the second ring.

"Hey, Kris. You finally ready to talk?"

I can feel the tears starting to well in my eyes. "Not much to say, really. You know what happened?" I hear him take a breath and let it out loudly.

"Yeah, I do. He called me the next morning, telling me how much he fucked up. We had no idea you'd even been there until he found your clothes in the bathroom. Kris, I'm sorry he did this to you. I know that doesn't mean much, but I don't think he ever meant to hurt you, not intentionally."

I wipe the tears that are streaming down my face. "It doesn't matter if it was intentional or not. He did it. I get sick thinking about it. You should know how I feel. You walked in on Stephanie and that guy. I just sat there and watched. I couldn't move."

"Wait. What do you mean you watched?"

I take a deep breath. "I was sitting in the chair in the hotel room, waiting for him. Brian had called to let me know about what time he would be there. I went in the bathroom and changed into one of my dresses. I came back out to wait, and I heard him at the door with a woman. They came in and he was kissing her. Another one was behind them with her hands all over him. He ordered one girl to strip and get on the bed, while he had the other girl suck his dick. The one on the bed wanted him to snort something off her pussy, can you believe that? I was just...frozen. I finally got up to leave and heard one of the girls ask who I was. I looked back and he was looking right at me, and he said I was nobody. Nobody, Derek! How could he do this to me? I fucking loved him and he did this to me!"

I can't hear if Derek is saying anything else. I'm sobbing too hard and I can't catch my breath. I hear the door open and Mallory's there, wrapping me in her arms, making soothing noises. I guess she picks up my phone and talks to Derek, but I have no idea what she says. She just keeps holding me.

I guess I cried myself into exhaustion, because the next thing I hear is a deep voice in the other room, talking to Mal.

There's a soft knock on the door and Derek comes in. He takes me in before moving to the bed, and he too wraps me up in his arms. "I'm so sorry, Kris. So sorry you're hurting. Want me to kick his ass?"

I let out a watery laugh. "You can't do that. You're his best friend."

"Hey, I'm your friend too, and I don't feel bad for him right now. He got his own ass in this mess. I still can't believe it."

I can't either. All I can think of is what did I do to drive him to other women? I know we hadn't seen each other in months, but it hasn't been the first time. But what if this isn't the first time he's done this? How many others have there been?

"I don't think he's done this before, Kris."

I look up into Derek's face. "I said that out loud?"

He nods. "I'm not going to excuse what's he's done, but I think this was the first time."

"What about the drugs? They were all high as kites! Has he been using? I know y'all drink after the shows, but drugs?" I just can't wrap my head around it.

"We've always stayed away from the drugs. God knows there's enough of them backstage, but we never wanted to fall into that trap. I don't know what happened that night. Hell, neither does he. He can't remember a thing after the show."

"Well I can remember enough for the both of us, I promise you that. I see it every time I close my eyes." I hear Derek's phone ring. He grabs it, looks at the screen and runs his thumb along the bottom.

"It was him, right?" He nods. "Please don't tell him where I'm at." I figure if he hasn't shown up by now, he doesn't know where I am. And Mal would never sell me out like that. The only reason Derek knows is because she talked to him during my crying jag. I still don't know what she said, but I'm glad she talked to him, and that he showed up here.

"Are you going to talk to him? You know we leave for Europe tomorrow and we'll be gone for four months," Derek whispers into my hair.

"I can't talk to him right now. I need to wrap my head around this before I can do that. Right now, it may do more harm than good. I really don't think I can forgive him. Cheating has always been one of those things that is unforgivable to me, but I never expected it to happen to me with Brett. I thought he loved me enough. Hell, he proposed right before y'all left. I just…I don't…I don't know what to do right now. Maybe the time apart will do us some good, put things into perspective."

I feel Derek squeeze me a little tighter. "Yeah, maybe it will."

We lay in the bed, watching TV and eating junk food, neither really talking. He watches another cheesy chick flick with me and lets me cry on his shoulder. He never pressures me to talk about it again, or try to make me see Brett's side. He just holds me and lets me cry. Eventually, he'll have to leave. He hasn't been home long from Minneapolis and he has to get ready to leave again, so he needs to spend time with his parents, and Brett's uncle Jake. "Thank you for coming by, it means a lot. I couldn't ask for a better friend. I don't want to drag you into the middle of this, though."

"You're both my friends, so I'll be in the middle regardless. I can be the shoulder you both lean on. I can see both sides and help both of you see the other's side." He kisses the top of my head and leaves with a goodbye. Damn, I wish he wouldn't go.

I get up and look at myself in the mirror. I look like something the cat dragged in. My face is all blotchy and my hair looks like a rat's nest. I've dripped ice cream on my shirt, and I can't even remember the last time I showered, so I decide to do that. I'm stronger than this.

I get in the shower and soap up my hair and the rest of me, then shave my legs. I feel a lot better. It's amazing what some hot water will do for you. I get out, dry off, and reach for the lotion. It's apple-scented. I feel the tears well back up, but I blink furiously to make them go away. I throw the lotion in the trash and walk out the door and throw on some clothes. I stick my head out the door.

"Mal? Do you have any lotion I can use?"

"Sure, what kind?"

"Anything but apple." I'll never wear apple again.

CHAPTER EIGHT

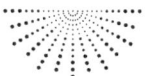

Kristen

It's been nearly four months since the guys left for Europe. I finally got out of Mallory's apartment and found my own place. Thank goodness, I still had some of my old furnishings in storage from when I had moved in with Brett. I couldn't go back there with the way things were. I went back to work and eventually started back to school for the next semester—my last semester; the most important one. I needed to be on top of my game. All I seem to do is work on the weekends and go to class and study during the week. I've even taken up CrossFit. It's helped me focus, and it's helped me lose the ten pounds I gained with my pity eating.

The pain has lessened, but it's still there. I try not to think too much about that night, and I haven't talked to Brett on the phone at all. It hurt too bad in the beginning, and now I don't know what I want to say. Maybe that makes me a bitch. I don't know. We've texted back and forth, and he sent me a long text explaining that night, or what he could remember of it. He told me how sorry he was and how much he loved me. But I can't believe it and I can't accept his apology. I don't know how I feel about me and Brett anymore. I'm still not over what he did, and to be honest, I don't know if I ever will be. Trust is a huge thing and I can't trust him.

I talk to Derek pretty regularly and he keeps me up-to-date with what's going on with the band and the sites they've seen. I think he may feel a little guilty that I talk to him and not Brett. The last thing I want to do is get between them, but Derek keeps reminding me that he's my best friend too. There's only a week before the guys come home, and I don't think I'm ready to face Brett. But it's coming, whether I like it or not.

I'm lying in bed, waiting for my alarm to go off. Why? I don't know. My bed is so comfortable. I actually slept through the whole night. Or, at least, I don't remember dreaming. My alarm beeps and I turn it off. What the hell was I thinking when I said I'd do CrossFit at five in the morning?

I put on my sports bra, leggings, shoes, and grab a tank top, then I'm out the door. Luckily, it's only a couple miles away from my apartment. I drink some of my pre-workout drink as I pull into the parking lot. I'm the first one here after Josh, our drill sergeant. Well, that's the way I see him. He's awfully flirty, unless it's time to work out. I had to set him straight a couple months ago, about being available. But I'm not sure what I am. Nevertheless, I head inside to see what the WOD is. Son of a biscuit eater. I hate burpees. They're the devil's spawn.

Camryn walks in and comes over to me. "Is he trying to kill us today?" she asks as she glances over our work out for the day.

"Maybe."

We start stretching as we wait for the others to come in. Josh rounds us up and gets us started. As Camryn and I start our run, she starts checking out Josh. "Sarge is looking mighty fine this morning. Do you think you could bounce a quarter off that ass?"

I look at her and laugh. He really does look good. He knows it, but he's not a jerk about it. "All right, ladies, quit laughing and run, or I'll add some more burpees." We shut the hell up and run.

We make it through our work out without dying. Camryn and I head over to the coffee shop for a hit of caffeine. "So, have you talked to him yet? He's gonna be back next week. You need to put yourself, and him, out of misery." One thing about Camryn, she gets right to the point.

"No, I haven't. I don't know what to say, and I can't forgive him. Not yet. Maybe never. Then where will we be? If I can't trust him, we can't have a relationship. But I know I have to make a decision soon." She nods her head in agreement. We spend the rest of our time drinking our coffees and talking about school. Camryn decided to go back to school with me. I think we're both crazy. We've got one more semester to go and we'll have our Master's Degree in Nursing and can sit for our nurse practitioner boards.

We part ways so we can get ready to go to lecture. Boring. I get home and head into my room to shower. I lay my phone on the table and it rings. I glance at it and see it's Brett. "Hi, Brett." He doesn't say anything for a few seconds.

"I can't believe you answered. God, I miss you so much, sweetheart. How are you?"

I sit on the bed and check the time. I have a little time to talk before I have to get ready. "Tired and sweaty. Just got home from working out with Camryn. How are you?" This damn small talk is killing me, but I don't know what else to say.

"Tired. It's been a long four months. We actually have the night off. I figured I was just going to get your voicemail again. Did Camryn come over and work out, or did y'all go take a class somewhere?"

"We're doing CrossFit a couple miles from my apartment." He doesn't say anything, then I hear him take in a sharp breath.

"Your apartment? What do you mean, your apartment? You moved out? When the hell did this happen?"

"Right after y'all left, Brett. I couldn't stay there. I needed some space to think. I mean, I told you I was leaving."

"I can't believe this. First you leave your ring on the table, then you move out. I just thought you left for a little while to stay with Mallory, needing some time."

"God, you are an arrogant fucking bastard, aren't you? Did you just expect me to go on like nothing happened? Sit around like the good little girlfriend, waiting for you to come home and try to justify why you fucked other women? Do you think you own me?"

"No, I don't."

"Good, because that sure as hell wasn't going to happen. I'm not one to sit around and feel sorry for myself. Do the poor, pitiful me act. I don't need you or your money. I know that you pay all the bills and I never had to worry about any of that stuff, but that doesn't mean you can control me or whatever. I make a good living doing what I do and I love it."

"Kris, damn it, I don't want to control you or own you. I love you. I pay for all our stuff because I can. It makes me feel like a man knowing that I can take care of you. I know you love your job. I would never expect you to just sit at home. Are we through? Is that it? Can you just turn off how you feel for me? Because I sure as hell can't. I love you, Kris."

"No, I can't just turn it off, you idiot, but I can't forget what you did either. I don't know if I can ever forget it or forgive you. You broke my fucking heart and I don't know if it'll ever be whole again!" I'm screaming at him over the phone. Tears are rolling down my face. "I just can't, Brett," I whisper and hang up the phone.

I throw the phone on the bed and head for the shower, wanting to wash away the tears that continue to flow. My stomach hurts. I feel bad that I yelled at him because that's so not me. I'm usually the level-headed one, the calm in the storm. But not this storm.

After my shower, I decide that I can't go to class. I never miss, but there's no way I can concentrate today. My head is pounding from crying. I grab my phone and see a text from Brett.

I love you. I will always love you, but you need to decide where we go from here. I know I fucked up and I can't change the past. You'll never know how much I regret hurting you. I want to marry you and spend the rest of our lives together. But it's up to you. I'll see you next week when we get back. I need to see you. I love you.

I sit on the bed, wrapped in my towel, as my wet hair drips water down my back. I feel the tears well and I blink to clear them before I text Camryn to let her know what happened, and that I won't be in class. She texts me back with a sad face, and offers to get the notes to me.

Getting dressed, I head to the kitchen and grab some ibuprofen for my headache before I sit on the couch to watch some mindless TV, because I don't know what I'm going to do.

CHAPTER NINE

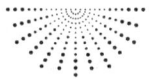

Brett

I hang up with Kristen, stunned. I can't believe she answered the phone, first of all. She's ignored every call I've made to her in the last four months. I was happy to hear her voice and not a recording, but then she dropped the bomb; she moved out of our house. Fuck, I guess I was being an arrogant ass, expecting her to be there when I got home, to our home. I may have bought it before we moved in together, but that house was ours. Her touch is everywhere. She belongs there. I guess I just didn't want to believe that she wouldn't be there when I came home. And when she started yelling at me? Damn. She never lets her emotions get the better of her. I guess it just shows how upset she is. It's killing me to know that I'm the cause.

I head to the minibar and grab a few of the bottles. I open them up one by one and down the contents, not even bothering to see what they are. All I know is that they burn on the way down. Finishing them off, I call downstairs and request a bottle of whiskey, then lay back on the bed and wait. I think back on the first time Kris saw the house that I bought. I had taken her house hunting with me because I knew eventually that we would get married and live there, together, so she needed to choose the house too.

We pull up to the house and step out of the SUV. The realtor had started out with the mini mansions, but I could tell by the look on her face that she didn't like them. This house is much more modest. Kris has a small smile on her face.

"This home is twenty-eight hundred square feet. It has four bedrooms, three baths, and a media room. It has an open floor plan and a gourmet kitchen. There is a three-car garage, swimming pool, and a storage shed out back. It sits on three acres. Please, take a look around." The realtor steps out the door and we start looking around. Kris eyes everything. When she walks into the kitchen, she stops and smiles wide.

"It's gorgeous." I grab her hand and head upstairs to where I assume the master is. Kitchens and bathrooms sell a house, right? I glance in a few rooms, but they don't look like a master bedroom. Finally, we get to the end of the hall. This is it. It's nearly twice as big as the other two bedrooms up here. It's open, with huge windows on one wall, and plenty of space for a king size bed. I walk her to the bathroom and hear her gasp. "This is gorgeous." It has a stand-alone glass shower with too many shower heads to count. There's a deep tub, split sinks, but where's the toilet? I spy another door and open it up. Oh, there it is. "I could soak in this tub and actually have the water cover me. I'm in heaven".

I chuckle. "I guess you like it, huh?"

She looks at me like I'm crazy. "Like it? I love it!" She walks out of the bathroom and looks around the room. She sees another door and opens it up. "This closet is huge!"

"So, you think I should buy it?"

"Hell yeah."

I grab her arm and pull her to me. I wrap her up in my arms and give her a quick kiss on the lips. "Okay, I'll get this one." I hold her close. "I want to make love to you in this room."

"But the realtor—" I hush her with a kiss and move my hands down her back to squeeze her ass. I love her ass. It's firm, and big enough for my hands. I stick one of my hands down the back of her jeans and under her panties, feeling her wetness as I penetrate her with my finger. She moans and clutches at my shoulders. I remove my hand and step back to unbutton her jeans. I pull them down, along with her panties, and slip them off one of her legs. She moves her hands down and rips at my jeans. I get them pushed down past my ass, along with my underwear, and she grabs my dick. She gives it a couple strokes and I can't take anymore. I lift her up and she wraps her legs around my waist. I walk us to the nearest wall and press her up against it. I grab my dick and line it up with her core, rubbing the head around the wetness. God, it feels good. But I need inside her pussy. "Babe, I love you," I whisper. I give her a quick kiss and she gasps as plunge my dick inside her. I give her a second to get used to me before I pull out, then I slowly push back in.

"Please, Brett, fuck me." And with that, I lose control, pounding her harder into the wall.

"I want you to come on my cock. I want to feel you squeeze all around me." I place my thumb in-between us and find her clit. Giving it a firm rub, she falls apart. She cries out and tightens around me, squeezing me tight. I thrust twice more and I'm lost. We're both gasping for air.

She looks me in the eyes and says, "I love you too, Brett."

I pull out of her and lower her legs. Shit, I wonder if there's anything to clean her up with. I leave her leaning against the wall and go into the bathroom. Luckily, there's still a roll of toilet paper on the holder. I grab a handful and head back out. "Give me that," she chuckles. I hand it to her and she cleans up, then heads into the bathroom with one leg still out of her clothes.

I chuckle and she turns around and sticks her tongue out at me. I think I hear someone on the stairs. I pull up my pants and tuck myself back in my briefs, just before the realtor opens the door. I can only assume the room smells like sex. She gives me the hairy eyeball. I just smile at her and say "I'll take it. We'll be down in just a minute." She huffs and shuts the door. I turn and see Kris standing in the doorway, her face beet red. "I love you."

"Love you too."

I moved into the house two weeks later. Kris helped me decorate and put her stamp on the house, then I finally talked her into moving in with me three months later. I can't imagine being in that house without her.

When I open the door for room service, I find Derek standing behind the guy. I take the whiskey, tip the guy, and walk back into the room with Derek on my heels. He's been as tenacious as a junk yard dog, trying to keep me on the straight and narrow.

"What's that all about?" he asks, nodding to the bottle I'm holding. I take off the top and take a healthy swig.

"I finally talked to Kris. She moved out of the house and she yelled at me. I think that calls for tying one on." I take another swig and look over at Derek; he doesn't look surprised. "You knew?" He nods. "And you didn't tell me?"

CHAPTER TEN

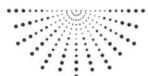

Derek

I see Brett take another swig of whiskey. "Yes, I knew she moved out. She told me a while ago. I just assumed she'd told you too. She told you she was leaving, right?" Damn, he doesn't know how often I talk to Kris. I think I've talked to her more than I have him lately. Should I tell him that I know how she's doing in school? How much she's enjoying her job? How much she's liking her CrossFit, and that her instructor likes to flirt with her? Nah. With the look on his face, I'm going to keep all that to myself.

"What did you expect, Brett? She left her engagement ring on the table for you to find. Did you think she was going to stay there after what you did? Sit at home like a good little girlfriend and wait for you to justify what you did?" I can't keep the anger out of my tone. I'm still pissed off that he cheated on her in the first place, even if he doesn't remember doing it.

"I don't really know what I expected, but it wasn't that." He rubs a hand through his hair and sits on the side of the bed. "It's just that, I love her so much, and I can't imagine my life without her." He takes another tug on the bottle. "What if I've screwed up so badly, I can't fix this? What if no matter how much I love her, my fucking up costs me the woman I love forever?"

I don't know what to say to him. I sit down beside him on the bed. "I don't know, man. I don't know if you can fix this, or if she'll ever forgive you. Put yourself in her shoes. What would you do if you walked in on her sleeping with another man, or two? Whether you remember or not, it happened. You can't change that. Listen, I know you never meant to hurt her, but the damage is done. When we get back, talk to her. Sit down face-to-face and work it out, or go your separate ways." I watch him put his head in his hands. I know it's hard for him to hear, but this isn't good for either of them. I'm glad she talked to him, even if it was just to yell at him. She needed to get some of her anger out toward him. I have a feeling it's only the tip of the iceberg, and it's going to get worse before it gets better. He looks at me with the saddest expression on his face, then takes a deep breath and nods.

We just sit there and pass the bottle back and forth between us; he's taking about three drinks to my one. I decide to call down for room service. Otherwise, we're going be sicker than dogs. Half an hour later, there's a knock on the door. Brett has polished off most of the bottle and is staring at the wall, so I answer the door and room service wheels in the cart. Grabbing a bottle of water, I twist off the top and hand it to Brett, but he just stares at it like he doesn't know what to do with it. "Drink it." I take what's left of the whiskey away before tipping the waiter as he leaves. I had ordered some sandwiches, thinking the bread could soak up some of the alcohol. I grab a plate and take it over to him. "Take a few bites and see if you can hold it down." I grab my own plate and start chowing down.

I watch some British comedy as we eat in silence, the I get up and get in Brett's bag and grab a bottle of ibuprofen, along with another water. "Take these and drink this, then get in the shower." He drinks the water and downs the pills. He tries to stand up, but wobbles, so I grab his arms and hoist him to his feet, holding him until he's steady. With a gentle nudge, he heads toward the bathroom. Once I hear the shower turn on, I grab some basketball shorts and boxer briefs out of his bag and toss them on the sink for him. I step back out before I see something I don't want to see. I've seen the guy naked before, and I don't want a repeat.

I watch some more TV and wait for him to get out. By the time he comes out of the bathroom, he looks a little better. "Get some sleep, man. I left some water and more ibuprofen on the table. Take them when you get up." He nods his head and gets under the covers. I head out of the room.

I had planned on heading back to my room, but end up in the bar downstairs. Saddling up to the bar, I grab the attention of the bartender. She's a pretty little blonde with a nice rack. I order a beer and she bends over to grab one out of the cooler, giving me a nice view of her cleavage. We chat for a bit in-between her helping other customers. After a while, it's just me and her. Her accent is sexy as hell.

We close down the place and she comes around the bar. I swivel on the stool so she can move between my legs. I take one last pull from my beer as she starts to run her hands up and down my chest. Placing the bottle on the bar, I grab the back of her neck and pull her face toward mine. Our tongues tangle together as I grab her ass. Breaking the kiss, I lean back and ask, "Wanna go upstairs with me?" She nods and bites her lip.

She's breathing hard, and her face and chest are flushed. I grab her hand and we head out the door. Once we get into the elevator, we're all over each other. When the doors open, we stumble out, almost not even making it to my room. I fumble with the room key while she's licking her way down my neck. When I hear the door beep, I turn the handle and pick her up, carrying her into the room.

Tossing her down on the bed, we both start to strip down to nothing. Once we're both naked, I climb on top of her and push her blonde hair off her face. Gazing into her eyes, I can't help but think how much they look like Kristen's. Wait. I can't think about her right now; it's just wrong. She pulls my head toward her and I begin to kiss her. Slipping my tongue between her lips, I enjoy the feel of her tongue against mine. I move my lips down her jaw and down to her neck, placing wet kisses as I go. I make my way down to her breasts and circle my tongue around her right nipple. Drawing it into my mouth, I suck gently at first, then increase the pressure. Hearing her gasp, I reach up and pinch her other nipple between my thumb and finger, giving it a little twist. As I continue to suck on her breast, I move my hand down her stomach to the small patch of hair on her mound, then skim my fingers between her lips and into her wetness, easing one finger into her core. Pure lava. I pull back and enter her with two and she arches her back. I put my thumb on her clit and circle around it, without actually touching it. "Please," she moans and clutches my shoulders with her hands. "Fuck me. Please, fuck me." I release her nipple with a pop and smile.

Reaching over, I grab a condom out of my wallet, when she

places her hand on my dick. With a firm stroke, she grabs the condom with her other hand. "Let me". She's efficient with the wrap. When she's finished, she leans back and spreads her legs as she trails her hand down her stomach to her pussy. I move in-between her thighs, line up with her core and plunge in. So hot. I sit there for a second to get my bearings, but she thrusts her hips up a little and I pull back, only to thrust into her again. It feels so fucking good. I begin to pound her into the mattress. She breathes out harshly, digging her nails into my back. "So close. Fuck me harder." I lift her legs up over my shoulders and split her legs wider. Deeper and harder I go. She screams out as she clenches around me, and I thrust a couple more times and groan out my own release, then lower her legs from my shoulders and flop down on the bed beside her.

We're both panting from the exertion. I take the condom off, tie it up, and put it in the trash can. She leans over and kisses my shoulder, then moves to get off the bed. She grabs her clothes and heads to the bathroom. Not long after, she opens the door and walks out, dressed. She makes her way over to me and gives me a quick kiss. "That was great, but my name's not Kristen, love." I watch her walk out of the room. Fuck.

CHAPTER ELEVEN

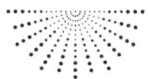

Kristen

The guys made it back home yesterday and I'm supposed to meet Brett at his Uncle Jake's bar in an hour. Being a nervous wreck would be a mild comparison to how I feel. I think I need to throw up. I've been thinking long and hard about our relationship, but I'm no closer to deciding what I want to do. I love him, but trusting him is something I just don't feel anymore. Every time he goes on tour, I would be wondering what he's doing.

I'm looking at the clothes on my bed, trying to decide what to wear. Do I try to impress him? Or do I go for comfort? I finally decide on a pair of black leggings, a long maroon tunic and a pair of sandals. I grab a long silver necklace with angel wings and slide it over my head, then pull my hair back into a low ponytail. Finishing off the look are my silver hoop earrings. I put them on and head out the door.

I walk in and see Jake behind the bar. He glances at me, smiles, and comes out, grabbing me up in a hug.

"I've missed seeing you, girl. How's it going?" We talk for a few minutes about my work and school, and some of the other band members come through the door. Jason and Isaac make their way over to us. Jason, the strong, silent one, grabs my hand and pulls me to him. The next thing I know, I'm in a hug, and it feels like I'm hugging stone. I guess I didn't realize just how much muscle Jason had. I feel his mouth by my ear and he mutters, "I've missed you." With one more quick squeeze, he lets me go. I'm then swept up into Isaac's arms as he twirls me around.

"Damn good to see you, Kris." He gives me a loud smacking kiss on the cheek and sets me down. I smack his arm and smile.

"I've missed you guys too. Did y'all have a good time traipsing across the globe?" They start telling me about all the places they visited and the sights they'd seen. In Isaac's case, it was all about the women. I never hear Jason talk about women. Sometimes, I wonder if he's batting for the other team. Not that I care who he bats for, but it would be a loss for the women of the world. I think he came back from touring even bigger, and I didn't think that was possible. Jason is the rock of the group, the one you depend on. Isaac, on the other hand, is the laid back, "go with the flow" kind of guy. I've never seen him with the same girl twice, and he definitely goes for the bimbo type— all body, no brains.

As we talk, I see sunlight come through the door as it opens. Brett and Derek walk through and my heart gives a little flip. Brett glances over and sees me, and so does Derek. He gives Brett's shoulder a quick squeeze and heads my way, drawing me into another hug. "Missed you, girl. You look a hell of a lot better than the last time I saw you. Y'all need to talk this out, okay? It's gonna be rough on both of you, but you gotta get it out." He moves his hands down my arms. "I can feel those muscles. Don't kick his ass, okay?" He glances over at the other guys and gestures with his head before he gives me a kiss on the head and walks away. Jason and Isaac follow, and Jake goes back behind the bar. I look at Brett and take a deep breath.

We meet each other halfway and stand awkwardly in front of each other. He looks into my eyes and pulls me into his arms, and I return his embrace. It feels like coming home, the way his arms feel wrapped around me, his cheek resting on my head. I lay my cheek on his chest and hear the steady beat of his heart. God, I wish things were back to the way they were before. Tears gather in my eyes. I try to ease my way out of his arms but he doesn't seem to want to let me go. "We need to talk." I step away from him and nod. He gestures with his head to a booth in the corner and we head that way. Luckily, there's not anyone else in the bar this early. He slides in one side and I slide in the other, facing him. Jake saunters up and gives Brett a bottle of Bud Light, and me a can of diet Dr. Pepper. He moves away as soon as he puts them down, then we sit in silence, neither of us knowing what to say or where to start. He reaches across the table and grabs my hand.

"I've missed you so much, Kris, and I don't know where to begin with this. I'm sorrier than you'll ever know."

"I miss you too, and I don't doubt that you're sorry. What you're sorry for is the question. Are you sorry you hurt me? Are you sorry you cheated? Or are you sorry you got caught?"

He closes his eyes and squeezes my hand tight. When he opens his eyes, they are glistening with tears. "Hurting you is the worst thing I ever could have done. You'll never know how sorry I am that I did this to you. And I'm sorry that I cheated. I've never, ever thought about cheating on you. I have no excuse for that night. It never should have happened."

I can hear the sincerity in his voice, but I just don't know. With my free hand, I reach up to wipe the lone tear that is running down my cheek. As soon as I do, another takes its place. "Brett…" I'm not sure what I'm going to say, but he cuts me off.

"Please, Kris. I love you." He reaches into his pocket and pulls out my engagement ring, placing it on the table. The diamond twinkles as the light hits it. "I want this back on your finger. I want you back in our home. I can't change what's happened. It's the stupidest, most fucked up thing I ever could have done to you. You have to know, deep down, that that's not who I am. God, I don't even remember what happened that night. I would never want to hurt you like this. I can't lose you, baby. You're everything to me." I pull my hand away from his.

"But you did, Brett. You've hurt me more than you'll ever know". The tears slide down my cheeks and blur my vision. He leans over, like he's going to wipe them away, but I lean back, away from him. I don't want him to touch me right now. I don't think I can bear it. I wipe my cheeks with the back of my hand as Brett leans back against his seat.

"And it tears me up inside that I've caused you this pain. Every time I think of what I did, and being the one who's making you cry, feels like I'm being stabbed in the heart. I can promise you that I'll never hurt you this way again."

"How do you know that? You don't even remember that night. What happens the next time? How can you be so sure that it will never happen again?"

"You can trust me." He takes a deep breath. "I can't live like this anymore, Kris. This is all up to you. I love you, and I want to be with you." He thumps his hand on the table, jarring me.

"I love you, but you destroyed everything we had. I mean, how many times have you done this to me? Have you been cheating on me the whole time, or just this tour?" I'm getting louder with every question.

Brett leans forward and places his arms on the table. "No. I've never cheated on you before, or on any of our tours. It was just a one-time thing—"

I cut him off. "How the hell do you know if it's the only time? You don't even remember that time, you say, but I sure as fuck do. I see it every time I close my eyes. I see that girl sucking your dick. I hear you telling the other one to strip. And I most definitely remember you calling me a nobody." I scoot out of the booth and stand up. I can't do this. I'll never be able to trust him again. I never want to go through this again. "I'm sorry, but we're through. Have a good life." I turn around and practically run to the door. I hear him call my name, but I can't look back. If I look back, I'll lose it, and I'm done with losing it.

CHAPTER TWELVE

Brett

It's been two months since Kristen walked out on me at the bar. I can still see the expression on her face as she yelled at me, the devastation that I caused her. Jesus Christ, how the hell could I have done this to her?

I reach over on the table to grab the bottle of Jack Daniels sitting there and glance at the clock on the table. It's a little after seven. With the sun shining through the window, I shade my eyes with my hand and take a drink. Shit. My head is pounding and my mouth feels like cotton. Something brushes against my leg, and I look over to find a brunette starting to stir. It takes me a minute to realize it's Tammy, the waitress from the bar. I vaguely remember bringing her home last night. I always use the guest room when I bring a girl home, but for some reason, I actually slept with her in my bed last night—Kristen's bed. Tammy blinks her eyes at me and smiles, but I don't smile back. "It's time for you to go. Did you follow me home last night?"

She has a little frown on her face, but nods her head. I move to get out of the bed. "Be gone by the time I get out."

I head toward the bathroom and shut the door, Jack still in my hand. I place it on the counter, take a piss, then pick the bottle back up for another swig. I turn on the shower and step into the freezing water to help wake me up and wash the skank off. Once I finally feel awake enough and get out, I grab a towel and move to the counter. Placing my hands on the cold surface, I take a good look at myself in the mirror. There are dark circles under my eyes, and my cheeks look sunken in. My chest isn't as defined as it usually is, and my ribs are noticeable. I guess that's what I get for living on a liquid diet. I grab the bottle and take another drink.

I finally make my way downstairs and find that Tammy has made herself scarce. Just as I clear the landing, there's a knock at the door. "Brett! You up? Open up, man!" Derek yells through the door. He pounds again. I slowly walk over to the door and open it.

"For the love of Christ, please, stop knocking. I have a headache."

He pushes open the door and I move out of the way to let him in. As I try to shut the door, something hits it and pushes it back open. Jason walks through, with Isaac following close behind him. I follow them into the kitchen and sit down at the island. Derek gets a glass out of the cabinet and fills it with water, then reaches in through another door and grabs a bottle. Putting the glass in front of me, he shakes out four ibuprofens. As I swallow them down, I see Jason grabbing stuff from the fridge, then moves to the stove and grabs a skillet.

"Make yourself at home," I mutter. Derek glares at me.

"What the fuck, Brett? Are you trying to kill yourself? Have you taken a look in the mirror lately?" I shrug my shoulders. No, I'm not trying to kill myself, but I'm not living either. I continue to sip on the water and a glass of orange juice is placed on the counter.

"Drink that too," Isaac says over my shoulder. "You need the vitamins." I pick up the juice and take a sip.

"What are you guys doing here?" I yawn and reach down and scratch my balls through my shorts. "Not that I mind y'all dropping in at the ass crack of dawn, of course." Jason sets a plate of scrambled eggs down in front of me, and my stomach rolls a little.

"Eat it," Jason says gruffly. I grab the fork and take a small bite.

"We're here because we're supposed to be in the studio at eight this morning. We decided to ride together, remember?" It does sound vaguely familiar. "I figured we'd have to drag your ass out of bed this morning. I was surprised you were already up and moving around."

"Yeah, I had to get rid of my company from last night," I mumble, and Derek stiffens beside me. I think he's taken mine and Kristen's breakup almost as hard as me.

"You're unbelievable." He turns around and walks out toward the living room as I dig into the eggs. As soon as I scrape the plate, Jason takes it away. "Get dressed. We need to leave."

I head upstairs and throw on some clothes. Luckily, Nelda still comes once a week so I have some clean clothes. I grab some briefs, socks, jeans, and a T-shirt. I pull them on and realize that my jeans nearly fall off my waist. I search for a belt and put it on. Once I'm dressed, I grab my wallet off the dresser and make my way down the stairs.

We load up into Derek's truck and head down to the studio. Brian had one built beside his house, which made it really convenient since he only lived about five minutes from my house. We really needed to work on some material for our new album. Derek has written a few new songs and I can't wait to get them recorded. I have a few song ideas in my head that I need to flesh out too.

We walk into the lounge area and Brian is there, standing with his arms across his chest. He hates it when we're late. "'Bout damn time y'all showed up! We got work to do. We only have a couple more months until the next tour starts, and I would like to get a few songs for the new album completed before we leave. Derek, we'll work on your stuff first." We start to move toward the back rooms. "Brett, hold up." I stop and let the others move on ahead.

I turn to look at Brian. "Yeah, man, what's up?"

"Take a seat, you look like shit. I'm not going to lie to you. I'm worried about you. You haven't been yourself lately. I know you've been struggling with the whole Kristen thing, but you have got to straighten up. This band needs you, and I need you to be at your best. I've heard how you've been drinking to excess every night. You've gotten as bad with the women as Isaac. Get it together, man." He pats me on the back and moves toward the control room. I can hear the guys warming up. Time to step up and be the leader of the Silver Tongued Devils.

WE WORK a few hours before we decide to take a break. Brian orders us Italian for lunch, which is one of my faves. As we all dig in, I realize what I've been missing. Between eating solid food and shooting the shit with the guys, I feel good. I've missed this. I see Derek glance at his phone, then sneak a quick look at me. He excuses himself and answers the phone as he heads out the door. With that look, I know he's talking to Kristen. And just like that, I feel like shit again. He comes back in and grabs his keys.

"I'll be back in a few. Isaac, why don't you work on that one rift and we'll finish it up when I get back." He heads out the door and I follow.

"What's up, Derek? What's wrong?" He stops in his tracks when he hears my voice. I can see his shoulders move with a deep breath before he turns around and faces me. "Kris's car broke down and she needs a ride to class." He turns back around and heads to his truck.

"Why the hell is she calling you?" I yell at his back.

He stops again and turns around. "She's still my friend, just like you are. I'm not gonna turn my back on her. I try to keep y'all in separate parts of my life so y'all don't have to see each other. I'm not willing to give either one of you up, and I still spend time with her. More than you know, since you're usually drunk and with some random chick. I don't like watching you spiral. I keep hoping you'll get over this funk. I know it's gonna take time, but I'll always be here for you." With that, he climbs in the truck, starts it up and pulls out.

CHAPTER THIRTEEN

Kristen

It's now been six months since I've seen or spoken to Brett. The first two months were hard because he was home, living in the house we shared. How I managed to pass my classes, I still don't know. Thank God for Camryn, who kept me on track. I found that if I worked all the hours I could when I wasn't in class, I could forget about Brett—for a little while, at least.

I even decided that it might be time to move on, go on a date. I finally took Josh up on his repeated attempts to ask me out. Camryn's favorite saying is 'The best way to get over someone is to get under someone else.' I don't know if I'm quite ready to go that far, but I'm going out tomorrow night with Josh.

The guys are due back from touring the West Coast on Saturday. I miss them. It's like another hole in my heart when they're on tour. The things I've seen and read scare me a little. Apparently, after I walked out on him at the bar, Brett decided to become a manwhore. Pictures are floating around the internet of him making out with a different chick every night. In most of the pictures, he looks drunk or stoned. I hope he's not using. He's so much better than that.

Even though I struggled through the last semester of school, I passed with a 3.7 GPA. Then I passed my boards, thank God, and got a job at a pediatrician's office. I had met Dr. Daniels at the hospital, and she had really encouraged me to go for my nurse practitioner's license. She told me that she could tell I had a real passion for helping children, and that if I went back to school, she would hire me to work with her. It has been a dream come true. Dr. Daniels is probably the smartest person I have ever met. I started working at her office a couple weeks ago, and it's been a whirlwind of activity, to say the least. Well kids, sick kids, paranoid parents—I've seen them all, and many of them. It's go-go-go from the time we open until we close, but I love it. I enjoy not working twelve hour shifts and having the weekends off. I finally saved up enough money to get a new car after mine had broken down for the sixth time. I know Camryn was getting tired of carting my ass around, so I ended up buying a Hyundai Tucson. It's a granite color with black rims and dark tint. I feel like such a badass as I zip through traffic, jamming out to Adelitas Way. It's been a rough day and I'm ready to get home to get into some comfy clothes and chill.

As soon as I pull into the parking lot, the guys' song comes on, and I realize the ache in my chest is barely even there anymore. I turn off the ignition and head into my apartment, change clothes, and put on a movie. Ghostbusters, my fave. It takes me back to the night that Derek and I spent watching it, after he found out Stephanie was cheating on him. That still gets me riled up. I just don't understand how you can care about someone and do that to them. The thought of her hurting him still ticks me off. Derek's a great guy, and she couldn't have done any better. He's sweet, funny, and a great listener. Not to mention, that hot ass body. Or that dark hair that's soft to the touch. His dreamy blue eyes. That beautiful beard. The industrial in his ear and the barbells in his nipples. I can picture him in my head from watching him when we would work out together. The sweat dripping down his back as he lifted those heavy weights. Muscles bulging, making the tattoos on his arms shift. Him catching me looking and giving me that sexy as hell wink. I shake myself out of my thoughts and realize I'm practically panting. My hand is down the front of my panties and I'm wet as hell. I snatch my hand out and sit up on the couch. Maybe I do need to get laid.

I get up and make a sandwich, then sit back on the couch and finish the movie. By the time it's over, it's late, so I head to bed.

Crawling under the covers, I hear the air conditioner kick on and smile. It feels so good to sleep with it cold. I just wish I had someone to cuddle with. But, instead of Brett's face, I picture Derek's. I'm still horny as hell. I reach in my bedside drawer and pull out my rabbit. Placing my hands under the covers, I pull off my panties and turn on the rabbit. Hearing the soft hum of my little friend, I place it near my pussy and slowly move it around the top of my mound. I start to picture rough hands moving on the inside of my thighs, moving closer and closer to my core. One of the hands moves up my stomach to my breast, gently cupping the entire thing and the thumb rubs across my nipple, while the other hand goes to my pussy. One finger dips into my heat, as if to test how wet I am. I feel one finger enter me with a gentle thrust. It retreats, then I'm filled up again with two fingers. I lift my hips up to allow them to go deeper. The hand on my breast pinches my nipple. "Please," I whisper. The fingers thrust harder, and I hear myself whimper. I'm so close. All of a sudden, the hands stop and flip me over onto my stomach. Gripping my hips tightly, they raise me to my knees. I feel him move between my legs and the head of his dick rubs small circles through my wetness, then he thrusts, hard. He begins to pound in and out as I grab the sheet in both hands and cry out. Reaching up, he wraps a hand in my hair and pulls my head back. The pain feels delicious. "Give it to me," he orders. With one hard thrust, I feel myself explode. He wraps his arm around my chest and continues to ride me until he stiffens against my back. With a gentle kiss on my shoulder, he moves his hand to my jaw and turns my face to look at him. All I see are blue eyes until I slowly come back to myself and turn the rabbit off. Damn, that felt good. I've never come so hard by myself. I don't know if I've ever come that hard at all.

I'm suddenly exhausted. I place the rabbit back in the drawer and the last thing I think of before I drift off is that I'll wash it in the morning.

I WAKE up the next morning with Derek on my mind. Damn, I have to quit thinking about him that way. We're just friends, and it's wrong. We don't feel that way about each other. I need to focus on Josh, but every time I do, he morphs back into Derek. I head to the shower to get ready for work. Half an hour later, I'm headed out the door. Maybe a busy day at work will help me forget about the way I was thinking about Derek.

· · ·

WE CLOSED EARLY, as Dr. Daniels was heading out of town, so I got off at three instead of five. Today was pretty relaxed compared to the rest of the week.

I'm heading home when my phone rings. I glance at the screen and see that it's Derek. Heat flames across my face. I hit the ignore button and keep my focus on the road because these people are crazy! I pull up to my apartment complex and head to the door. I haven't even thought about what I'd wear tonight. I change out of my scrubs and pull on a tank top and a pair of yoga pants. Heading into the closet, I pull out a few outfits and lay them on the bed.

An hour later, I'm still trying to decide on what I'm going to wear. I pick up the phone to call Camryn and ask her advice when I hear a knock at the door. I glance at the clock and see it's still too early for Josh to be here. Walking to the door, I check the peep hole and gasp. I throw open the locks on the door and pull it open. He smiles at me. "Derek!"

CHAPTER FOURTEEN

Derek

I actually got home a day earlier than expected. I am so ready to be home for a few weeks. We actually have a two week break before we have to head back out on the road. I hope after this last leg, Brian lets us have some time off; I'm getting burned out. So, instead of riding in the bus home, I hopped on a flight. The rest of the guys were still laid up in the bus when I headed to the airport this morning. During the flight, all I could think about was seeing Kris.

I pull out my cell and scroll through my pictures until I find one of her. It's one I took when she wasn't looking so I could make it her contact pic on my phone. She's sitting on a chair, outside, looking off in the distance. The sun is hitting her hair just right, making the long blonde waves glow, and she has a small smile on her face. She was watching some squirrels chase each other around the tree, and I remember thinking she was the most beautiful thing I had ever seen. I hear the captain tell us that we're about to land, so I put my phone away.

I disembark and head out of the terminal, making it outside just as my mom jerks the car to a stop. I can even hear her slam the car into park before she hauls ass out of the driver's seat. She runs over, throws her arms around me and buries her face a little north of my belly button. I seem to forget just how tiny she is. I hug her back. "Missed you, Momma."

She pulls away from me and gives me a big smile. "Missed you too, sweetie. Come on. Let's head to the house. I'll fix you some lunch."

"Fried chicken and mashed potatoes?" I ask with hope in my voice.

"What else?" She chuckles. We load up in the car and head home.

It's nice to be back in a place with peace and quiet. My dad and I remodeled the pool house behind their house, and that's where I live. It has an open kitchen, living room, bedroom, and a bathroom. What more could a bachelor ask for? I didn't see the point in buying a house or renting an apartment with us on tour most of the year, but I didn't want to be living with my parents either, so this was a nice compromise. I'm far enough away from the house so my momma can't spy too much, but still close enough that I can walk over for dinner.

I lay back on the bed and revel in the feel of my bed, stuffed full of Momma's fried chicken, mashed potatoes, green beans and rolls. I feel like I have a food baby. I glance at the bedside table and check the time. It's a little after three, so I decide to call Kris. I grab my phone and scroll through my contacts to her number. It starts to ring, but goes to her voicemail. I call the clinic where she works now and find out they've closed early for the day. Huh. Maybe I'll have to take a little drive.

I pull up to her apartment complex about an hour later. Seeing her new car sitting in her spot, I park and head to her door and knock. Maybe I should have tried to call again before I came over, but it's too late now. I hear movement on the other side of the door, then the locks disengage and the door flies open. Holy shit! I think she's gotten prettier since the last time I saw her. Her hair is up in a messy bun. She's wearing a tight blue tank top with no bra, and gray pants that fit her like a dream. I smile at her.

"Derek!" I open my arms and she jumps in, wrapping her legs around my waist. I clutch her to me and kiss her temple.

"Damn, I've missed you, Kris." She gives me a tight squeeze, then stiffens. We both realize we're in an intimate embrace, not that I mind. She loosens her grip on me and I set her back on her feet.

"What are you doing here? I thought y'all wouldn't get back until tomorrow sometime?" She grabs my hand and leads me into her apartment and we take a seat. Damn, she looks good.

"I decided to fly back instead of taking the bus. I needed a fix of my momma's fried chicken." I laugh, and she chuckles too. She knows how good that fried chicken is.

"So, whatcha doin' tonight? I was thinking maybe we could order in a pizza and watch a movie." She looks down and starts to twist the bottom of her tank top, raising it just enough that I can see her belly button and something silver. She has her belly button pierced? Since when? Damn, that's sexy. I glance up to see her looking at me, chewing on her bottom lip. That's a sure sign that she's nervous.

"Well, actually…" She clears her throat and looks me in the eyes. "I have a date tonight." Wait, what? A date?

"I didn't realize that you were seeing someone." I feel a little pain in my chest.

"We're not dating. This is the first date. He's one of the instructors in my CrossFit class. He seems like a nice guy, and Camryn's advice is that I need to get under someone else." She blushes as she says it. "Not that I have any plans for that to happen tonight, of course. I'm not a one-night stand kinda girl, ya know?" I can feel myself getting angry. Get under someone else? Like hell! Is this what jealousy feels like? I stand up and pace in front of the couch. "Do you think it's too soon to start dating? It's been nearly a year since Brett and I split. He's obviously moved on, hundreds of time, I'm sure. Don't you think it's time I did the same?"

How I feel right now has nothing to do with Brett; it's all me. I want to be the one she gets under, and that's so wrong. They may not be together, and he may be fucking anything with a pulse, but we have the bro code. You don't go after your friend's girl, or ex-girl in this case. But I can't help how I feel. "No, Kris. If you're ready to move on, then it's time."

She beams at me. "Thanks. I guess I needed to hear someone besides Camryn tell me that. Wanna help me decide on what to wear tonight? I know it's not your thing, but I can't decide. Guess that's what happens when scrubs take up ninety percent of your wardrobe." So, for the next half hour, I get to watch her model clothes. It's pure torture.

I leave about twenty minutes before her date arrives, but I don't go far. I sit in my truck, parked off to the side where she can't see me. As I wait, I finally see another truck pull into the space beside Kristen's ride. A tall, muscular blond guy gets out, then reaches inside to grab some flowers. Jesus...flowers? Really? He heads to the door and knocks. After a few seconds, Kris answers the door. She's left her hair down, and the porch light makes it look like a halo from where I'm sitting. She's wearing the outfit I helped her pick out. Little does she know I picked the one that covered the most skin and gives off the 'I'm not easy' vibe. I'm glad that she decided to wear it.

He hands her the flowers and gives her a kiss on the cheek. I feel my blood pressure rise. She heads back in with the flowers and is back moments later. Glad to see she didn't let the fucker through her door. They head to his truck and he makes sure to open the door for her. She lifts herself in and I can see him check out her ass. His eyes better be the only thing on her ass tonight. They pull out of the parking lot, and I watch until his tail lights disappear. I want to follow, but that would be a little stalkerish, so I start up my truck and leave. There's a little Mexican food place just up the road from her apartment complex. I'll head there and stuff my face until I decide my next move.

CHAPTER FIFTEEN

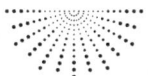

Kristen

The date started out okay, and the flowers were a nice touch. We went to see a new scary movie that was out, but he kept trying to talk to me through it. I hate that, but I guess a movie isn't so great for a first date, especially if I don't want to talk or be distracted. He held my hand, but I felt nothing. Nada. No spark. Just his sweaty palm. After the movie, we went to one of the chain restaurants. I have to give him props, though. He's been a gentleman. I try not to cringe when he places his hand on the small of my back as he opens the door for me to go in first.

Thanks to call ahead seating, we get led to our table pretty quickly after we arrive. Now, normally, I eat pretty damn healthy, and I work out five or six days a week. But tonight, I decide to splurge and get a small steak and a loaded baked potato. As I give my order to the waitress, I see Josh give me a strange look. Thinking maybe what I ordered is too expensive, I decide to offer to buy dinner since he paid for the movie.

"How about I pay for dinner, since you paid for the movie and popcorn?" I ask.

"No. I asked you out tonight, so I'm paying for it all. I guess I've never seen a girl eat so much." Excuse me, what? Did he really just say that to me? I glance down, not even sure how to respond to that.

There's an awkward silence that falls between us after that, so I try to break the ice by asking the usual questions. What type of music do you normally listen to? Country, unless we're working out. Did you grow up around here? Yes. Did you go to college locally too? Yes. Where? UNT. What did you major in? Kinesiology.

The conversation is stopped by the arrival of our waitress with our food. Thank goodness. This is a train wreck. I didn't really pay attention when Josh ordered, so I look at his plate to see what he ordered. Grilled fish, a ton of broccoli, and a huge mound of brown rice. Okay then. That doesn't look appealing at all. He whips out his phone and starts to type something out. He looks up and sees me looking at him. "I have to enter my macros." His what? I guess the question is on my face and he goes into a long-winded explanation of how many macros he can have a day: calories, fat, carbs, protein. Jeez, I didn't know a diet could be that complicated. He goes on about how he's in a bulking phase since we're going into the colder months. Then, he'll be in a cutting phase. He starts to describe his weight lifting regimen, in addition to his cardio. The whole time he's talking, I'm steadily eating my delicious steak, baked potato, and asparagus. After a little while, he starts to sound like the parents of Charlie Brown.

I glance out the window and see a truck parked outside that looks like Derek's. I can't tell if it's his because it's kind of in the shadows, away from the nearest light. I remember back to when he first bought his truck.

"Come on, let's go mudding!" Derek yells as he comes in the house.

"What are you talking about? Mudding in what?"

"Let me show you." We walk outside and I see his new jacked up Chevy Silverado. It's so pretty. It's shiny black, with a four-inch lift. He's had bars added to help us shorter people climb in. Behind it, he's pulling a trailer with a new Polaris RZR. Holy moly! It looks awesome.

"Hell yeah! Let me change and we'll go." I run back in the house and pass Brett. "Go check out what Derek bought. We're gonna have so much fun!" I haul ass upstairs and change into one of my old T-shirts, ripped jeans and old shoes. I'm going to get muddy and enjoy it. I head back down the stairs and we head out. The truck has leather seats and a bad ass sound system. I don't know if I've ever been this high up off the ground before. We crank up the radio as we fly down the road.

We had so much fun that day. We had actually had a pretty good storm the day before, so the ground was plenty wet. We headed out to Derek's parents' land and tore it up. I can't remember a time I had had so much fun. We ended up covered in mud, so we had to go back to his parents' house to shower and change. I ended up having to borrow some of Derek's clothes to wear home.

"Are you listening to me?" I snap my gaze up to Josh's. I guess he noticed that my attention had wandered away from him.

"Sorry, Josh. I guess I zoned out for a second there." I look at his plate and notice he's barely touched his food. "How's your food? Mine's delicious." And it is. I've almost cleaned my plate. He makes a gruff sound and begins to shovel his food into his mouth, and I mean shovel. I've never seen someone who eats like him. I don't even know if he's chewing. Or breathing. In a matter of minutes, he's cleared his own plate.

"You know, you really shouldn't eat that much fat and carbs at the same time, Kristen. It's hell on your metabolism. I've noticed that you've been slacking at the box too. Maybe you should come work out with me, I hit the gym twice a day. Build up some of your muscle mass." He keeps talking, not even really looking at me. Who the fuck does this guy think he is? I discreetly signal the waitress. She gives me a slight nod when I mouth the word "Check."

I interrupt Josh and excuse myself from the table and head back to the bathroom. I need a minute. I use the facilities, wash my hands, and make my way back to the table. The waitress is there and Josh is talking to her, then I see him slip her a piece of paper. Wow. He's slipping the waitress his number. He's a real stand-up guy. The waitress turns around and spots me, and her eyes go wide. She can't really move without going by me. She tries to move past me, but I stop her with a hand on her arm. "You're welcome to him, hun. Just watch what you eat in front of him." She looks at me like I'm crazy as I let go of her arm. I get to the table and ask Josh if he's ready to go. He nods his head and we head for the front door. I barely give him time enough to catch up with me before I'm in his truck, buckling my belt, while he gets in on his side.

"Anywhere else you wanna go?"

I shake my head no. "I'm kinda tired, and it's been a long week. I think you should just take me home." He gives me a quick look and we pull out of the space. We're silent on the way back to my apartment. We don't even have the radio on to serve as a buffer.

After what feels like the longest drive in history, we finally pull into my apartment complex. He turns off the truck, gets out, and rounds the truck to open the door. He offers me his hand to help me out and I hesitate, but after a moment, I slip my hand into his. He leads me to my door, stops, and looks at me.

"Are you gonna invite me in?" he asks. Is he for freaking real? I want to laugh in his face, but that would be mean.

"I don't think that would be a good idea, Josh. It's late." I turn to unlock the door when I feel him grab my arm and turn me back around.

"You sure about that?" He moves in, trying to kiss me, but I turn my head and his lips land on my cheek. He pulls back, looking at me questioningly. Then, taking the hint, he says good night. I don't even watch him go to his truck as I unlock my door and go in. Thank goodness that disaster is over. I kick off my shoes and hear a knock at the door. Please, don't tell me he came back.

Opening it, I find Derek leaning against the door frame. "Let me in, Kris." I move to the side and he hurries through, stopping in-between the couch and TV. Closing the door, I turn back around and Derek's there. He's so close, you couldn't put a piece of paper between us. "Kris," he whispers. He raises a hand and places it behind my neck, then pulls me forward and kisses me.

CHAPTER SIXTEEN

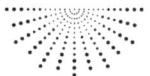

Derek

I feel like a fucking stalker or something. I ate a dozen tacos and nursed a few beers to kill some time. I still ended up at her apartment complex, waiting for her to get home from her date. It feels like for-fucking-ever before I see her date's truck pull up. He gets out and goes around to her side, opens her door, and I see her hesitate for a second before she gives him her hand. I wonder what happened tonight to make her hesitate? They walk to her door, exchange words, then he leans in for a kiss, but she turns just in time for it to land on her cheek. I grip the steering wheel tight; so tight, my knuckles turn white. He turns away to head to his truck, and she goes in to her apartment as he slams his door and hauls ass away. Before I even realize it, I'm standing at her door, knocking. What the fuck am I doing?

She opens the door. "Let me in, Kris," I say. She nods her head and slowly opens the door. Once I'm standing in her living room, I think to myself, now what? As she closes the door, I walk up behind her. When she turns around, we almost touch. "Kris," I whisper. Before I know it, I have a hand on the small of her back and the other on the back of her neck, drawing her slowly to me. I place my lips on hers and gently kiss her, then pull back and look at her.

I dive back in, slipping my tongue in-between her lips, just a little to test the waters. She opens her mouth a little more, letting her tongue dance with mine. When she moans, I grip her hair in my fist and move my other hand down to palm her firm ass. Bending at my knees, I lift her up and she wraps her legs around my waist. She feels wonderful in my arms. I move us toward the couch and I sit down with her straddling my hips, making my dick rock hard.

"What are we doing, Derek? Are we crazy?"

"I don't think we're crazy, Kris. I've been thinking about this for a long time. Every time I've talked to you on the phone, I've felt like we've grown closer. I've been attracted to you from the get-go. You're a beautiful woman." She blushes and tries to look down, but I lift her chin so she has to look at me. "Like I said, you're beautiful, and it's not just on the outside. You have a beautiful heart and soul. I think I started falling for you a little that night I came over after Stephanie and I broke up. I thought it was a little crush and I would get over it, but I haven't. I can't. I want you. It may not be right, but it can't be wrong either." I pull her head back toward mine and kiss her. Hard. I'm the gasoline and she's the match. I run my hand up and under her shirt, splaying it across her back so I can press her chest into mine. I sit up a little on the couch and it makes her lean back a little, breaking our kiss. "If you don't want this, tell me now."

I can see the indecision in her eyes, but she shocks me when she lowers her hands to the bottom of her top and slowly raises it up, like she's teasing me. I can see the ring in her belly button twinkle. Her top clears her breasts, bringing me face-to-face with her lacy blue bra that almost matches her eyes.

I move my hands to cup her breasts, which fit my hands perfectly. I look up into her face as she places her hands on my shoulders. I push them together and kiss the exposed skin, then gently bite her nipple through the lace. She gasps and presses her breast closer to my mouth, so I move my hands around her back and unsnap her bra. Leaning back, I slowly lower the straps from her shoulders. She blushes and lowers her eyes. "No, look at me." She gives me her eyes and I move back to her breast. Lifting it up with my hand, I circle my tongue around the outside of her nipple. With each pass, I get closer to the tip. I finally reach it and gently take it between my teeth, then move to her other nipple and do the same thing. I let her nipple go with a pop and blow air on it, causing goose bumps to break out over her skin. I bend her slightly backwards with one hand on her back, and the other on her chest. She braces her hands around my neck as I start to make my way down her stomach. I lower my hand from her chest to the top of her jeans and slide my finger under the waist band.

"Kris, you still with me?"

"Yes," she moans, and that's all I need to hear. I put my hands on her hips and move to stand from the couch. She squeals a little as I stand up and clutches my shoulders tight.

"I got ya. Don't worry". I carry her into the bedroom and lay her down with her legs dangling over the side. I never realized how the height of a bed could be an advantage. I kneel between her legs to kiss her stomach again, and as I get to her belly button, I give the ring a tug. Popping the button of her pants, I pull down the zipper and lift her hips. I try to decide if I want to take her panties down right now or tease her some more. I leave them in place for now and work her jeans off her long legs. Kissing her ankle, I work my way up her leg with soft kisses. The closer I get to the heart of her, the more she squirms. I gently lower her leg back down and move both my hands to her inner thighs, running my thumbs slowly on the outside of her pussy lips.

"Please," she murmurs. I spread her open and lick around her clit. She tastes fucking delicious. I lick her from her clit down to her hole, gathering the wetness on my tongue as I slowly insert my finger. She's so damn tight. I add a second finger, then a third. I reach down with my other hand and open up my jeans to allow my dick some breathing room. I continue to thrust my fingers inside her and palm my cock, stroking it slowly as I feel her start to tighten. I lick her harder, faster, until she cries out, arching off the bed while she clenches around my fingers. I slow my thrusting and allow her to ride it out. When she relaxes I stand up, grab my wallet and pull out a condom. I hold it with my teeth and look at her lying on the bed, panting. Taking my jeans completely off, I roll the condom along my dick. When she opens her eyes, she looks at me, dazed.

"Are you ready, baby?".

She shakes her head yes and I move back between her thighs. I grip my dick and circle around her wetness. She's tight, and I am not a small man. I slowly push my way inside her, maybe a couple of inches, and pull back out. I push again and give her a little more. When I pull out, I thrust again, burying myself balls deep. I give her a second to adjust, but that's it. I place my hands beside her head, pull out, and thrust back into her, hard. I feel my balls slap her ass. I look into her face to make sure I don't see any signs of pain, and once I see she's fine, I begin to move inside her, pumping myself in and out of her.

"Harder, please!" I raise up on my knees and spread her legs wide, shoving into her without mercy. "God, yes! That's it. Don't stop doing that." Her pussy is hot, and so tight, I can feel my release filling my balls. With every thrust, she grunts loudly and starts to clench around me. I drop one leg and dip my finger in her wetness as I rub her clit. She goes stiff, clamping down on my dick like a vise. I can barely move, it feels so fucking good. I only manage two more hard thrusts before I roar out my release.

We're both breathing hard, and once I catch my breath, I slowly pull out of her, instantly missing her warmth. "I'll be right back." I go to the bathroom and dispose of the condom and clean up. When I walk back out, she's laying exactly how I left her. She tries to sit up, but seems to be having a time of it. I move to help her up and give her a kiss once she's steady on her feet. She gives me a shy smile and heads to the bathroom.

I sit on the side of the bed, figuring she's going to feel a little awkward. But, she surprises me. She walks out in all her naked glory, right to me, and kisses me. I climb in the bed, straighten the covers, and she crawls in, cuddling into my side. I turn the light off and wait until she goes boneless against me and her breathing evens out. Placing a kiss on her head, I can't help but think that this has been the best night of my life.

CHAPTER SEVENTEEN

Kristen

Blinking my eyes, I slowly come awake. I can't remember the last time I slept so well. I glance over at the clock on the table to see it's after eight. Guess that means no CrossFit for me this morning. It's probably for the best, though. I don't want to face Josh after that disastrous date last night.

Last night. What the fuck did I do? Have I lost my ever-loving mind? Just as I'm thinking this, Derek pulls me tightly against him and kisses me on the shoulder. Shit, I don't know what to do. I won't lie, the sex was amazing, but talk about an awkward morning.

"Good morning," he mumbles. He sounds sexy with his rough, morning voice.

"Morning," I mumble back. We lay there, neither one of us saying a word. I don't know what to say or how to act. As if he can sense my inner conflict, he gives me another quick kiss on my shoulder and gets out of bed. I wasn't prepared for him to get out of bed naked. Well, duh, of course he's naked. I need to get my head on straight. I watch as he walks to the bathroom, his back muscles and ass flexing. I can feel my pussy flutter. He is one sexy man.

Sitting up, I see his shirt lying on the floor and I quickly reach over and grab it before he walks back out. I don't know if I can face him without clothes. I slip the shirt over my head and take a quick whiff. God, it smells good, like his cologne. I sit and try to gather my thoughts. Caffeine. I need caffeine. Maybe that will help me get my act together this morning. I head to the kitchen and start a pot of coffee when I hear the bathroom door open. I keep looking at the kitchen counter, needing the nectar of the Gods before I can face him. I feel him more than hear him, move into the kitchen behind me. The heat of his body warms my back.

"Any of that for me?" he asks. I nod and clear my throat.

"Would you grab a couple mugs from the cabinet and my creamer out of the fridge, please?" With a quick kiss to the top of my head, he moves away. I feel the loss of his heat immediately as he moves to the fridge. I'm still too chicken shit to look at him yet.

He sets the mugs on the counter beside me and leans his butt up against it with his arms folded over his chest. "I was hoping this wasn't going to be awkward, but I think that's unavoidable, don't you?" I nod my head and look back to the coffee maker. Once the beeper goes off, I grab the mugs and fill them up. Unlike me, he takes his straight black. I hand him his cup, and to keep myself busy, I grab the creamer and take my time fixing it just the way I like it. I'm trying to figure out what to say. Raising the mug to my lips, I bless whoever invented coffee.

Figuring it has to be done, I slowly turn to face Derek. "I don't know how this could be anything but awkward." I look into his beautiful blue eyes. "But I don't regret a damn thing that happened last night." I hold my breath, waiting for his response.

He takes my cup and places it down on the counter, along with his, and slowly pulls me to him. "I don't regret a damn thing about last night either. My only regret is that I didn't do something about this sooner." He bends down and kisses me. He tastes like coffee—delicious. Pulling me tighter to his body, he wraps his hand in my hair as he works over my mouth. With my arms around his neck, I lift my legs and wrap them around his waist. The next thing I know, he's lowering me onto the table. When the cold wood touches my ass, I realize I don't have underwear on. He runs his hands up my thighs to my hips, and notices the same when he rubs his thumb along the side of my mound. He moves his lips down my jaw, toward my ear, and gently bites down on my lobe. Shudders run through me. It feels so good.

His hands move to his T-shirt and he raises it up my torso. I reach my hand up to his well-defined chest and run it over his right pec, circling my finger around the barbell at his nipple. I guess he likes that because he groans. He places his hand on the small of my back, and the other one, he runs down between my breasts. He pulls me forward along the table, planting himself firmly between my thighs as he continues to rub his hand up and down my chest, like he's learning the feel of me. "Your skin feels like satin, but I miss the smell of apples." Face close to mine, he places his nose in the crook of my neck and inhales deeply. "You're supposed to smell like apples." I'm too far gone to even know what he's thinking about. He raises his head closer to mine and takes my mouth in a rough kiss. I've never been a huge fan of French kissing, but he's definitely changing my mind.

He starts to move his hips, spreading open my pussy. I can feel the rough denim abrading my clit. I'm so wet, I can feel my juices running down my ass. The hand on my chest gently forces me back so I'm resting on my elbows. He kisses down my neck to my chest and places soft, wet kisses on the tops of my breasts as he squeezes them. "You're killing me," I whisper.

He gives a small chuckle. "Babe, you ain't seen nothin' yet." He clamps his teeth on my nipple and pulls. I gasp and arch my back toward him and that delicious pain.

"Please, Derek," I whisper. He allows me to sit back up. I rub my hand down his pecs to his stomach, to the top of his jeans. Moving two fingers between the denim and his skin, I rub my fingers across the head of his dick, feeling the precum on the tip. Using both hands, I unbutton his jeans and slowly lower the zipper. His dick practically jumps out when I part the material. I'm not the only one who forgot underwear. I wrap both hands around him and gently squeeze, causing him to moan. I lower one hand and cup his balls while giving him a firm stroke.

"Just like that, baby. It feels so good." After a few more pumps, he puts his hands in my hair and gently forces my head back to look up at him to take my mouth. That's the only way to describe how he's kissing me. I let go of him and move my hands around below his jeans to cup his ass. It makes his jeans sag a little, so I push them down over his hips. He pulls away from me so he can step out of them.

"Lean back," he whispers. Again, I recline on my elbows as I watch him kneel between my thighs. He spreads me open and glides his tongue along my clit. He makes slow, sweeping passes with the flat of his tongue from my hole to my clit. It feels so good. He circles my pussy, then fills me with his fingers, curling them as he moves in and out, hitting a spot no one else ever has. I can feel my orgasm building.

"Please, please, please," I chant. One hard thrust later, I shatter. The room darkens and all I can feel is my heart pounding as my orgasm ebbs away. The next thing I feel is the stretch as he powers into me. His big dick feels so good. I lose the fight, trying to stay on my elbows, and lay back on the table. He thrusts twice more and stops.

"No," I cry out. I raise my hips to encourage him on, but he pulls away. Instead, he flips me over until my chest and stomach are resting on the table, and uses his legs to work mine further apart. With one hand on my hip, the other on my shoulder, he thrusts back into me. He's so much deeper at this angle. With every thrust, I hear a little keening cry, and realize it's me. "Please, Derek, harder," I pant. He thrusts so hard, we move the table across the kitchen floor. I can feel myself building again. He must feel it too, because he takes the hand that's on my hip and moves it around to my mound, rubbing my clit with his fingers. The hand on my shoulder moves to my hair and he pulls. That's all it takes—I'm gone. All I can do is lay there on the table. One more thrust and he pulls out. I can hear him working himself, then I feel the warm splashes across my lower back and ass. He leans over me and presses his chest to my back. His weight pushes into the table, but it's not too heavy.

When we finally get our breathing under control, he stands up and helps me from the table. Taking my hand, he leads me to the bathroom and turns on the water. Once the temperature is where he wants it, he steps inside the shower, pulling me with him. Grabbing the body wash, he begins to lather me up, making sure to wash every spot. "You're going to smell like a girl after this," I say as I smile at him. He smiles and shrugs. Once he rinses me off, he makes quick work of soaping himself up as I wash my hair. I turn off the water once we finish, and we step out. Grabbing a towel, he begins to dry me off, placing small kisses along my shoulders.

"What are we doing, Derek? I mean, this is crazy."

"Crazy or not, it feels right, doesn't it? I know it feels right to me. We may have jumped the gun a little last night, but I wouldn't change anything. Right or wrong, I've been falling for you for a while now, and I don't see that changing anytime soon. If there's any chance for me and you, I'm gonna grab it with both hands." I melt at his words.

We head into the bedroom and dress, but I'm suddenly feeling awkward again. "It's funny. Lately, it seems like I can't get you out of my mind. Even when I was out last night, you were who I thought about. Hell, I can't even get myself off without thinking about you." I slap a hand over my mouth. I can't believe I just said that! I cannot be any more embarrassed than I am at this moment.

CHAPTER EIGHTEEN

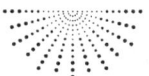

Derek

She turns away from me, like she's embarrassed at what she just admitted to me. I think it's hot as hell, and it's nice to know I'm not the only one who's been feeling this way. I have to adjust myself in my briefs. I walk over to her and wrap my hands around her waist, pulling her back against me. I look up and see our reflection in the mirror and take a deep breath. I'm glad to know it's not just me.

"How about we just take this slow for now. We can just hang out. You know, Netflix and chill stuff." That gets me a chuckle. "Or, how about we head out to my place. We can watch movies, eat some of Mama's leftover fried chicken, take a ride on the ATV. If you think we're moving too fast, we can slow this down. But I'm not going to back off. We can keep this quiet for a while if you want to, but I'm not going to treat this like some dirty little secret. We're gonna be in town for a couple weeks before we have to head back out. The guys and I will be in the recording studio most of the time, but I want to spend time with you while I'm here, go on dates and stuff. I realize we may have some resistance, so we'll have to decide if we think we're worth it or not. I want to give us every chance to make this work."

She nods her head in agreement. "Me too."

We decide to head to my place, so I throw on my clothes from yesterday and she puts on something more appropriate, as she wants to ride on the ATV. We load up in my truck and head out.

Rolling up to my place, beside the garage, we head straight for the ATV. There are plenty of hills and dips that we can get some airtime on. I start off slow to make sure she gets used to riding again. Now granted, this is not a Speed Demon, but if you hit some of those hills at a good amount of speed, you will get some definite air. She gives a girly squeal every time we go airborne.

It's been nearly two hours just riding around outside. It's great that she's a girl who likes the same things I do. We finally head back to my place. I check the fridge, and sure enough, it's stocked with leftovers from yesterday. Hell, I think Mama may have fried a whole 'nother chicken. Dishing up a couple plates, I pop them in the microwave. Kris heads to the fridge, grabs a beer and hands it to me. "None for you?"

She shakes her head. "No. I think I need to keep my wits about me today. I'll just have water, since you don't have any diet Dr. Pepper."

"No, I don't keep any of that girly shit in the house." I chuckle.

We sit down to eat, and she moans with the first bite of Mama's chicken. "Told you that shit was good." She nods in agreement, steadily cleaning her plate. I like to see that she's not afraid to eat in front of me, and she can put away some food. But her body is banging. It's even better since she started doing CrossFit, whatever the hell that is.

After we finish eating, we clear the table and she helps me do the dishes. Actually, she insists. I would have left them there for later. We head into the living room to watch a movie. Both of us agreeing on Die Hard, we sit on the couch and she snuggles into me. I can't for the life of me remember having a better day.

Since I know she wants to take this slow, I take her home that afternoon. "Do you have any plans for tonight?" I ask as she opens her door. She shakes her head no. "Then I'll pick you up at seven." I give her a quick kiss and walk back out to my truck.

I head back home, feeling like a million bucks. I know this can have some pitfalls, but to me, it's worth it. I just have to find a way to make this work and not lose my friendship with Brett. As soon as he crosses my mind, I feel a pang of guilt. This was his girl before he fucked it up; the love of his life. He still hasn't gotten over their breakup. He's been in a downward spiral ever since she told him she couldn't forgive him. So, should she and I be miserable because of that? I'm going to have to figure out a way to break this to him. But, I'm not going to tell him right now. No sense in stirring shit up if it's not going to work out between us. However, I don't see that happening. I have to remind myself that they've been done for nearly a year. It's not like I'm coming between them. Brett did that all on his own.

I pull up to my house and see Jason's truck sitting there. Fuck, I completely forgot the guys were due back today. I rack my brain, trying to think if Jason and I were supposed to meet up. Maybe being with Kris has fried my brain. It sure felt like it when I was coming inside her. I park next to his truck and he climbs out.

"Hey, man, what's up? How was the bus ride home?"

"It sucked balls, that's what it did. It seemed like the bus ride took forever. I'm damn glad to be home." He looks at me, questioningly. "Listen, I gotta ask you a question. I was headed over here a little while ago and passed you as you were leaving. Now, tell me if I'm wrong, but I seem to have seen a certain blonde all cozied up next to you in your truck. Tell me, Derek, what the hell are you doing?"

Well, fuck. I didn't want to answer questions about this, not until Kristen and I were in a committed relationship. I kind of shrug my shoulders at him. "Let's go inside. This conversation is gonna involve alcohol."

AFTER I TELL Jason the whole story, he sits quietly, thinking over what I've just told him.

"What about Brett?" he finally asks.

"I don't know what I'm going to do about this yet. I've been slowly falling in love with this girl. Coming between them has never crossed my mind, but he fucked up. I do feel guilty, but I'm not going to let that stop me. I'm not going to tell him right away. Truthfully, I'm scared to tell him. Who the hell knows how he's going to react? He hasn't been the same Brett we all know since we got back. I feel like I don't even know him. He fucks every groupie he can, and I can't remember the last time he was sober. He's got to be on something. He looks like shit."

"I know what you mean. I'm worried about him, about all of us. Brett was always the heart of the band, but now it's like we're coming in second after the pussy and booze. Maybe, since we're back from touring, Brian can have a talk with him. Something's gotta give, and I don't think you and Kristen are going to help the situation."

"I know, man. I don't know how he's going to react. That's why I was going to keep this quiet while we were home. But, I don't want to keep it a secret it if turns into something more. I don't want her to feel like she's some dirty little secret I have to keep. Dammit, it's just a fucked up situation. For now, we're going to keep it between us. We'll talk with Brian and see where it goes. I do think we need to get a handle on Brett before something bad happens, like something he can't recover from, or the band can't recover from."

"Okay. I'll keep quiet about this for now, at least until we try to get Brett straightened out. I just don't want this to send him down a hole we can't get him out of."

And I agree. I sure as hell don't want to hurt Brett, but this could be mine and Kristen's only shot at happiness.

Jason finishes his beer and heads out. I know I have a lot of thinking to do. But first, I have a date to get ready for.

CHAPTER NINETEEN

Kristen

I'm still kind of nervous about the whole situation, yet I can't deny today has been one of the best days I've had for as long as I can remember. I definitely got butterflies in my belly when he said he'd be here at seven to pick me up. I walked back into my apartment, sat on the couch, and stared at the TV. I still don't know what the hell we're doing, but I agree with Derek. This might be our only shot at being happy, together.

I have a few hours to kill before he'll be here to pick me up. So, I'll work on cleaning my apartment. It also helps me to think. But even after two hours of deep cleaning, I still don't have any answers. Ugh! I need to get my head on straight and think about this rationally, weigh the pros and cons. But not right now.

I keep getting texts from Josh, telling me how sorry he was for the way he acted, that he was being a jerk and wanted to go out again. I just roll my eyes. Does he really think he has a chance in hell of a second date? Even if I wasn't with Derek right now, that guy totally blew it. I texted him back, letting him know that all was forgiven, but I didn't think we would work out. I purposely left out any mention of Derek so there wouldn't be any drama.

I glance at the clock and realize it's time for me to start getting ready. He had texted me earlier and said to wear something comfortable. I have no idea what his plans are, but I know I'm excited to spend some more time with him. I decide to wear a pretty blue top, jeans, and some comfortable boots. I'm just finishing up putting on my earrings when I hear the knock at the door. I feel the rush of excitement, knowing I get to see him again. I hurry to the door and fling it open. "Brett?" I clear my throat. "What are you doing here? I really wasn't expecting you to drop by."

"Can I come in?" I open the door further and he enters.

"Um, just give me a second." I run to the table and grab my phone, shooting a quick text to Derek to let him know that Brett's here. I don't want him walking into an awkward situation. Setting the phone down, I turn back to Brett. He looks like crap. I don't know what happened to the man I fell in love with, but that man is not who I'm looking at right now. I take him in from head to toe. His once glossy hair is now flat. His complexion is sickly, and he's definitely lost weight. He looks like half the man I used to know.

"Not that it's not nice to see you, but I didn't expect you to drop by. What's going on?" I try to keep my distance from him without it being too obvious. It feels really strange to have him here.

"I just needed to see you, Kristen. I don't know why. It suddenly hit me today. I still don't like the way things went down between us. I know I can't change it, and I can't make you forgive me or trust me." He looks so sad standing there. I want to hug him, but I squish that thought quickly.

"Oh, Brett," I sigh. "I've forgiven you, but I just don't trust you with my heart. That may make me a bitch, but I can't help the way I feel. It would just hurt both of us. I do worry about you, though." Especially after seeing him now, in person. I guess he has been partying as much as it was implied. I was kind of hoping that things weren't as bad as they are. I feel guilty that I'm the cause of this, the cause of his downward spiral into whatever the hell this is. "I don't know what to do, Brett. Why did you need to come see me?"

"I just missed you, I guess. I needed to see your face, hear your voice." He takes a deep breath. "I still have your voicemail messages on my phone, just so I can hear you. Your pictures are still on my phone." How the hell do I respond to that? We stand there, awkwardly. I honestly don't know what to say. I shuffle my feet and bite my lip.

"Well, I guess it's time for me to go. I never meant to hurt you, Kristen. I hope you believe that." He looks so sincere.

"I do." He walks over to me, grabs my hand and looks me in the eyes. All I can see is the sadness in his and it breaks my heart. He lowers his head to mine, but I move, so he kisses my cheek. I look up at him, and he has a small, sad smile on his face. "Goodbye, Kristen." He turns and walks out the door.

I sit down on the couch. I don't know what the hell just happened, but it worries me. I'm afraid things are going to get worse before they get better. I grab my phone and text Derek to let him know that Brett just left. I don't think I feel like going out anymore, though. There are too many thoughts racing through my mind, and I have a sick feeling in my stomach.

There's another knock at the door, and I check to see who it is this time. I barely have time to open it before Derek has me wrapped in his arms. "I was already in the parking lot when I got your text. It took all I had to stay outside. Are you okay?" I nod my head, but then I start to cry. He just holds me to him until I soak his shirt. With a small sniffle, I lean back.

"What's happened to him? He looks horrible. I barely even recognized him. I didn't do this to him, did I?" I want him to tell me it's not my fault, but when I look into his eyes, I don't know what I see. Pity? Guilt? I don't know if I want him to answer now. My heart starts to pound and I can't breathe.

He cups my face with his hands. "Stop. Breathe, Kris. It's not your fault, but I can't say it doesn't have anything to do with you. To say he hasn't taken your breakup well is an understatement."

Derek takes my hand and leads me to the couch and we both sit down.

"I hope you don't mind, but I really don't feel like going out tonight. Can we just stay here?"

"Of course we can. I'll just order us some pizza and we can watch some movies. I think it's a great idea."

He gets the pizza ordered and we turn on the movie. I can't concentrate on it, though. All these thoughts are swirling around in my head. I know the breakup was rough. Not just on him, but on me too. Maybe in the beginning, I wanted him to hurt as much as I did when he cheated on me. I never wanted this for him. To think that drugs and alcohol were the answer. Now all I want for him to be is happy, because I'm feeling happy with Derek. We finish eating and the movie ends. Derek moves so we're facing each other. I can see that whatever is on his mind is bothering him.

"I've been worried about him for a long time. It seemed like the first month after y'all broke up, he was sad, but he still held out hope. Within a short period, he just started to spiral, picking up random chicks. He started drinking a lot more too. These last couple months though..." He takes a deep breath and lets it out. "I can't remember the last time I've seen him sober. And I don't think he's just drinking. I talked to Jason yesterday, after I brought you home, about this. We're going to get with Brian and let him know how concerned we are. Something needs to happen before Brett does something we can't fix. He needs help, but I think we need to be cautious about how we approach it. That's one of the reasons why I don't mind keeping quiet about us, but I won't keep quiet forever. And just so you know, Jason knows about us."

At my questioning look, he says, "Jason was coming to see me yesterday when we were leaving and saw us in the truck. He confronted me about it when I got back home, but he's agreed that it's for the best we keep it quiet." He looks into my eyes, and he must see something there.

"This is not your fault, Kris. I don't blame you for breaking up with him, for not being able to trust him again. It's not on you for how he's reacting to the situation. He had a choice, and he chose to drown himself in pussy and booze. I know you were hurt too, but you didn't decide to drink away the pain, or hop on to the next available dick. Everyone has free will. This is what he chose."

He pulls me closer until I'm lying with my back to his chest, in-between his thighs. Just being next to him makes a certain calm flow over me. I feel myself relax into him.

Sometime later, I feel him shift, and then he's picking me up. I look up into his face and he's smiling down at me. He carries me to the bedroom and sits me on the side. "Anything in particular you want to sleep in?"

"Your shirt," I say, and one side of his mouth quirks up. He strips off his shirt and tosses it to me. I begin to take off my top, but he stops my hands.

"You okay with me staying tonight? Or do you need some time?"

I reach my hands to his face and bring him closer to me, kissing him softly on the lips. "Please, stay with me."

"No place else I'd rather be."

He stands up and toes off his shoes. Removing my top, I pull his T-shirt on. He reaches down and unbuttons my pants and pulls them down my hips. "Go do what you need to do so we can go to bed."

When I finish in the bathroom, he heads in after me. I climb in under the covers and wait. He's out quickly and climbs in beside me, gathers me to him and kisses me on the lips.

"Good night, Kris. Sweet dreams."

CHAPTER TWENTY

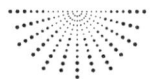

Derek

Kristen and I ended up spending all of Sunday at her apartment, just chilling out. Jason and I have been texting back and forth about when we're going to talk to Brian about Brett's behavior. We finally set up a meeting for tonight to talk.

Kristen looks at me. "Are you sure this is the way you need to go about this? Kind of sounds like an intervention. Is he that far gone?" She starts to bite on her lower lip. It's her tell when she's nervous.

"I'm afraid if we don't take the bull by the horns now, it will get that bad, and that's the last thing we want. Brett has been my best friend since we were kids. I hate seeing him this way. We're only going to talk tonight and come up with a plan." When she nods, I give her a kiss on her forehead and head out the door.

. . .

BRIAN, Jason, Isaac, and I agreed to meet at the little Mexican food place up the road. I walk in the door and see that I'm the last one to arrive, so I pull up the only remaining chair. The waitress walks over and I place my order for some tacos and another round of beers.

"Okay, guys. I know we've all noticed how Brett has been acting lately. Well, not just lately, but for the last few months. It's not getting any better. As a matter of fact, it's only getting worse." Nods come from all around the table. "I can understand him needing to get with any pussy he can. You know the old saying, 'To get over someone, you need to get under someone else.' I think we can all agree he's taking that to the extreme. I think he's taking the manwhore title away from Isaac." Isaac gives a small smile. "But now he's hardly ever sober. I think we can all agree it's not just alcohol that's the problem. Some of those lowlifes he's been hanging with have to be supplying him. I'm afraid if we don't do something soon, he's going to hurt himself or someone else."

Jason looks around the table. "Brett's been our friend for a long time, and some of us before the band." He nods to me. "And some of us since we formed the band. Brett has always been the heart of us, but now we're just coming in second."

Isaac looks at Jason, then me. "If Brett's taking away the manwhore title from me, then I think we can say he definitely has a problem. I think I've seen him a couple times, buying some shit off those guys. I tried asking him about it, and he just blew me off and changed the subject. When it happened, we were already getting ready to go on stage and I didn't have a chance to ask him again, then I forgot. That makes me feel like shit. Maybe if I would have stayed on his ass, we wouldn't be in this right now." He picks up his beer and takes a long drink and slams it back on the table. "Why the hell didn't I stay on him? "

The waitress walks up and begins to place our plates on the table. "You might wanna bring us another round, darlin'. I think it's gonna be a long night," Jason informs her. She nods and hurries away, but not before throwing Isaac a sexy grin, which he doesn't even seem to notice. Interesting. Or maybe he's wrapped up in self-loathing right now.

"It's not your fault, Isaac. It's all of us. I think we saw what we chose to." He looks at me and nods.

We dig into our food and exchange some small talk, throwing around ideas for songs, writing lyrics, and staging for music. Most of the night, Brian doesn't say much. "Brian, what do you think we should do at this point? This has just as much to do with you as it does with us. If it wasn't for you, we wouldn't be where we are today. We all look up to you. You're as much a part of this band as each of us."

Brian slowly peels the label off his beer bottle, then looks around the table, making sure to make eye contact with each of us. "I love you guys. You're more than just a band to me, you're family. To see one of my family struggling like this weighs heavy on my heart. Not only because he's hurting himself, but he's hurting us all, as a family and as a band. Professionally, this could hurt us. If he continues down this path, he's not going to be dependable. Y'all are the band, but he's the face. He's the one who's most recognizable. If he starts to fuck up, it could ruin us all. Personally, he has the potential to destroy this family. I'll move heaven and earth to try and prevent that."

My food sits heavy in my stomach. I guess in the grand scheme of things, I wasn't thinking about what it could do to us professionally. Of course, I never thought music would be my profession forever. I always figured I'd end up in construction with my dad. So when we hit it big, it was an exciting thing. Now, to think it could all come crashing down is a blow that I didn't expect.

"I think we need to sit him down and talk with him, like an intervention. But I don't want to give him the ultimatum of us all walking away. I just want him to know that we support him and that we love him. He needs help, but I don't know if he realizes it or not. Hell, he went to see Kris last night." Jason looks at me sharply. "She didn't say much about it, but it did upset her. We all know this path started after they broke up, but it's been nearly a year. And the way he's going about getting over her is just hurting him."

Brian stands up. "We're supposed to meet at ten in the morning at the studio. We can have some breakfast brought in and just sit and talk like a family. Maybe that'll get us started on the right track. I don't think we'll be lucky enough for him not to fight us on this, or agree to get help right away. It may take some time. We do have another tour coming up, so if you boys will excuse me, I'll start getting things set up. Y'all have a good night."

I glance over it Isaac. "You're awfully quiet tonight. I expected it from stone face over here." I gesture toward Jason, who gives me the finger. "But not you. Something on your mind besides this?"

Isaac takes a couple minutes, like he's trying to think of what he wants to say. "It's this and something else. Both are weighing heavily on me. I think we've got a good game plan for Brett. Now, I just need to figure out what I'm going to do about my other problem."

"You having women problems?" I chuckle and take a swig of

my beer. He doesn't say a word and drains his own, then signals the waitress for another. "What the hell, Isaac? You never have women trouble. Or, is it just one in particular?" Isaac nods his head. "Did you knock one of the groupies up?" He chokes on the drink of beer he just took.

"Fuck no! I haven't knocked anyone up. I'm just way out of my league on this one. One chick? For me? I never would have thought that would happen. If you ever would have thought I'd be upset over one girl, I would have laughed in your face. But I can't get her out of my head. Scared she's burying herself inside my heart."

Jason looks at him. "Who is it?" Straight to the point for old stone face.

Isaac shakes his head. "I'm not ready to go there yet. As much as I want us to be a couple, I don't think she's ready. Listen to me, a couple? A relationship? God, I never thought I'd hear those words come out of my mouth." Isaac takes another swig of beer. "They have any hard liquor in this place? I think I need it."

Jason looks over at me and points to me with his bottle. "Do you wanna let your cat out of the bag?" I give him a look that says he better shut the hell up.

"What's he talking about?" Isaac asks me. "You got something you need to let out too? You having woman trouble of your own?

I debate on telling him about me and Kristen, but I decide against it, at least for now. "No trouble, really. I just don't want it out in the open. Not right now, but soon."

Isaac looks at Jason. "How about you, man? I see that little hickey on the side of your neck. You got you a woman on the side?" Damn, is he blushing?

"Nothing to talk about." He finishes off his beer and sits the bottle down. He pulls out his wallet and throws down some cash. "I'll see you boys in the morning." He turns and heads out the door.

Isaac gets up too. "I have something I need to do tonight. I'll catch you in the morning." He throws down some cash and follows Jason. "You good to drive?" I holler at him. He gives me a little wave and is gone. I finish my beer and check my phone. Kristen texted me, wondering if I'm coming back over tonight or heading home. I text back that I'm going to run by my place and get some stuff, then I'll be over. I'm spending all the time I can with her. I get up, pay the check and head out to my truck.

CHAPTER TWENTY-ONE

Derek

Monday morning came way to early. I guess I didn't realize that Kris went to CrossFit before the sun even thought about coming up. I remember her asking me to go with her, but I think I fell back to sleep before she finished asking. I woke up again a few hours after she left. Apparently, she already snuck back in, got ready for wor, and left again. I walk into the living room, running my hand through my hair and yawning. I spy a piece of paper stuck to the coffee maker and head that way. Have a great day! Xoxo, Kris. I can't help but smile as I pour a cup of coffee and get ready to head out.

I text Jason, Isaac, and Brett to see if we're going to hit the gym before we go to the studio. For us, keeping in shape helps us keep the female fans just as interested in us as our music. Jason and Isaac hit me back pretty quickly with affirmatives. Nothing from Brett, though. I'm already wearing my work out clothes so I head to the gym. Since I'm the first to arrive, I go in so I can start stretching. After a few minutes, Jason and Isaac stroll through the doors. I check my phone, but there's still no reply from Brett. "Y'all heard anything from Brett?" Negatives from both of them. It's been a while since Brett has joined us for our work outs. It's one of the things we've always done as a group or in pairs for as long as I can remember. Before music became our job, Brett and I stayed in shape working for my dad's construction company. "Well, if he doesn't show up by the time y'all stretch, we'll start without him." They nod and get ready.

Instead of texting, I call Brett. It rings a few times and goes to voicemail. "Hey, man. Just wondering if you were going to join us at the gym. Don't forget, we're supposed to be at the studio at ten. See ya." I put my phone away. "What's first? Weights or cardio?" They both moan at cardio. Ha! Weights it is.

We finish up with the work out a little over an hour later. Damn leg days are a killer. Occasionally, I can still feel my leg muscles quiver. We hit the showers and get changed to head to the studio. I hate that we can't hit the sauna today, but we're out of time.

We make pretty good time and arrive a few minutes before ten. We head in and can smell the food as soon as we open the door. Brian always treats us right. "Damn, this looks good! I'm starving! Our work out was a killer." We all grab a plate and load them up. Brian's housekeeper is the one who keeps us fed when we're around, but no junk food for us. She tries to keep us on the straight and narrow. Brian likes to have healthy meals and works out just as much as we do. For an older guy, he's in really good shape. He can probably keep up with us, no problem.

"Did Brett work out with y'all this morning?" he asks as he fixes himself a plate.

"No. I texted him, but he never responded. They said they hadn't heard from him either. I tried to call but he didn't answer, so I left him a voicemail. I did leave on there a reminder that we were to be here at ten. Hopefully, he'll roll in soon."

"Well, it's only a little after ten. I'll give him a few more minutes before I start calling."

By the time we finish our food, its half past the hour and Brett still hasn't shown up. Brian tries to call his cell, and I call his house. No answer on either. I try his Uncle Jake, who informs me that he saw him last night, completely wasted, along with the night before. He also says that Brett left with Tammy, the waitress, last night.

"Maybe I should go check his house." I stand up to leave.

Brian stops me. "No, we all go. We handle this as a family. We'll just have a talk with him there. Let's go."

We all head outside and get into Brian's SUV. The ride to Brett's house is quiet. I'm afraid of what we will find when we get there. Hopefully, he's just sleeping off last night. We pull up into Brett's driveway and see his truck parked in the yard, not the driveway. Fuck, I hope this doesn't mean he drove home drunk. I don't see Jake letting him drive home intoxicated.

We head up to the door and it's not even latched. I knock anyways, but don't hear anything. We walk in and the house is trashed. Clothes are thrown about, lamps are knocked over, beer bottles poured out. We head up the stairs. Opening the bedroom door, I find more of a mess than downstairs. It looks like a tornado went through it.

Brett's lying in the bed, and he's not alone. I can see two

different hair colors on the pillows besides his. I walk over and reach over a redhead and shove him on the shoulder. Nothing. God, I hope he's breathing. I shove him a little harder. "Brett!" Nothing. I shove him a little harder and he rocks back into the brunette on his other side. "Brett!" I yell. He finally jerks a little bit and raises his head. I've woken the other two along with him.

"Am I dreaming?" the redhead says, trying to be sexy. She looks like shit. "Four more sexy guys to play with us." She reaches a hand toward me and I step back. "Sorry darlin'. We ain't here for you. Why don't you get up and get moving." She moves to get out of bed and throws the covers back. She makes a big show of stretching, thrusting her breasts out and arching her back. She sees that none of us are interested, huffs, and slowly bends down to grab some clothes, trying to show off her ass.

"Move!" Jason barks. That does it. She's out the door before I can blink.

Tammy hugs herself all up on Brett's back while Brett looks at us, wide-eyed, like he doesn't have a fucking clue about what's going on. "You too, Tammy. Get out."

"Maybe Brett doesn't want me to leave. Ever think about that? We're good together and he knows it. That's why he keeps coming back for more."

Jason steps up to the bed and glares down at her. "Maybe you need to get your ass outta here. Maybe he keeps coming back 'cause you're feeding his habit. Don't think I don't see those track marks on your arms, honey. You need to keep your druggie little ass away from Brett. I'll be sure to mention this to Jake. He'll fire your ass in a heartbeat. Now get the fuck out."

She hops out of bed, mumbling under her breath. She grabs

something and heads out the door, naked. "I've already called them a cab," Isaac says as he puts his phone away. "Someone may want to head downstairs and make sure they don't steal shit." Jason heads out the door. I can just picture him standing down there with his tree trunk arms crossed over his chest, stone-faced.

Brett still hasn't moved. He's just staring at us with an unnerving stare. I snap my fingers in front of his face. He blinks, then focuses on me. "Whatcha doin' here, Derek?" He blinks his eyes a few times.

"You guys wanna head downstairs and start a pot of coffee? I'm going to get him in the shower and sober his ass up." Brian heads out the door. Isaac moves over by me and we get Brett in to a sitting position. We lead him to the bathroom and wrestle him into the shower. At least with him being naked, we don't have to worry about undressing him. We get him situated on the bench where he can lean on the side wall. I want to turn the water on cold, but I'm afraid that may be too much for his body to handle right now. I position the shower heads where they will hit him and turn the water on lukewarm. After a couple of minutes, he's more awake. He's able to finish the shower by himself and we head out, but I leave the door open just in case. I grab Brett some easy clothes to put on for when he gets out, then strip off all the bedding and lay the clothes down. Brett comes out of the bathroom with a towel wrapped around his waist.

"What are you guys doing here?"

"Well, when your sorry ass didn't show up at the studio this morning, we got worried. Called the house and no one answered. We decided to drop by and make sure you were okay, and from where I'm standing, you sure as fuck are not okay."

Fuck. I rub my hands through my hair. "Get dressed and meet us downstairs. We need to talk." And with that, I turn around and head down the stairs.

We're all waiting for Brett to make his grand appearance. Coffee's been made and Jason has made some scrambled eggs and toast. I can hear him coming down the stairs at a slow pace. I look around at everyone in the kitchen and make sure we don't look like we're about to jump his ass. Brian's on his phone, talking to someone, while Isaac is on his phone, playing a game. Jason is sipping on a cup of coffee and drumming one hand on the counter. I had grabbed a guitar out of Brett's music room and I'm softly strumming it.

"Morning, guys. Sorry I overslept. Y'all didn't have to come all the way over here, though." I look up as Jason slides him a cup of coffee across the island counter top. Brett looks like hell. Even worse than the last time I saw him four days ago. Dark circles under his eyes. Sunken cheeks. Dull eyes. It looks like he's lost at least twenty pounds. His chest isn't as defined. He still has a six pack, but it's because he's lost weight. I can see his ribs. Even though he's trying to hide it, he's winded just from taking a shower, getting dressed, and coming down-stairs. How the hell did I miss this? How did I not see what he's been doing to himself? Man, I'm a shitty friend. I glance at the other guys and see that they've all come to the same real-ization.

"Brett, we need to talk. We've watched you over the past few months fall further and further down this hole that you're in, and we're bad friends for not realizing how bad it has gotten. Did you drive home drunk last night?" He has a blank look on his face, like he doesn't remember. "Because the way you parked your damn truck, it sure as hell looks like you did. There's a nasty dent in the fender. So, I really hope you didn't hit some-one. What is going on with you, man?"

He looks at me with remorse. "I don't know. I guess I didn't realize it was this bad. I don't even remember coming home last night. Jesus, what am I doing?"

"That's the same shit that got you into this, if you'll remem-ber. At first, it wasn't that bad. Sure, you were drinking more than you had been, but it wasn't affecting the band. But as more time has passed, you've gotten worse. I can hardly remember a time that I've seen you sober. When you didn't even come to the studio this morning, I knew we needed to do something. We had to come over here to find you because we were worried, and I don't think you were just drinking last night, were you?"

Brett won't even look me in the eye, or any of the other guys. He just rests his forearms on the counter and looks down. "No, it probably wasn't just alcohol last night. Tammy gave me something—a pill—and I don't remember too much after that." He looks up with tears in his eyes.

"I can't believe you're doing this. And driving under the influence? That's totally not you. That was one of the things you and I swore would never happen after your parents' acci-dent. We made a pact that we would never do to a family what those drunk drivers did to you. I don't know who you are anymore, but I love you. The guys love you. So, we're going to get this shit straightened out." I blink back tears.

Brian walks over to us. "Maybe, while we're home, you should come stay with me. To be honest, Brett, you look like hell. You look like you're strung out. I don't think you're quite there yet, and we sure as hell don't want you to be there. You'll come stay at my house. No drinking, no drugs, no pussy. As a family, we will work on straightening you out."

I glance down at Brett and see that he's crying. "I guess I didn't realize how bad I'd gotten. It's a good idea for me to come stay with you, Bri. I need to get my head on straight."

Isaac steps up. "So, what the hell happened this weekend to make you go off the deep end?"

He takes a deep breath and lets it out. "I had it in my head to see Kristen. I don't know why. It was like all I could focus on. So I stopped by to see her Saturday night. I was surprised that she didn't slam the door in my face. Even more surprised she let me in. I think it gave me a little hope." He wipes his hands up and down his face. "I could tell how awkward it was for her, but I had to let her know how I felt, to let her know how much I missed her. It wasn't like it was before. There was no comfortable silence. I tried to kiss her, and that's when I realized it's over for her. I guess when I realized I lost her for good, it just sent me over the edge. I didn't care anymore. I ended up at Jake's because I knew he wouldn't let me do anything too stupid. Apparently, that didn't work out too well last night. I was right at the edge of a cliff, but I'm glad I've got you guys to help me from going over that edge."

I feel a pain stab me in the chest when he talks about Kristen. I'm glad that he's realizing it's over between them, but I feel guilty as shit because I'm in love with her. Jesus, I'm in love with her. I glance at Jason and see him looking at me. I know what he's thinking, about how me and Kristen being together might send him spiraling out of control. We'll just have to keep that under wraps a little bit longer, until he's more stable.

"Okay, here's the plan. Brett, head upstairs and pack some clothes. Is Nelda coming over today? Because this place is a pigsty." Brian starts to take charge. At Brett's nod, Brian continues. "We'll go easy at the studio today. You're probably gonna be on house arrest for the next couple weeks, until we leave for the next tour. You'll go work out with the guys every morning or with me. Like I said, no alcohol, no drugs, no pussy. You're gonna be a damn choir boy. I think that should get you straightened out. But don't think for a damn minute that I won't be watching you like a hawk when we go on tour this time."

"I really appreciate this, guys. It's nice to know that you have my back. " Brett's voice cracks as he speaks. He goes to each of the guys and gives them a hug, then stops in front of me. "And you, man. You're my brother. What would I do without you? You've been there for me, always. My rock. We may not be blood, but we have the bond of brotherhood. That will always be the tie that binds us. Brothers forever." We hug and I scoot back.

"Get your ass upstairs and get some clothes packed. We have an album to make."

He heads up the stairs, and I brace my arms on the counter. Brothers forever. God, I hope so. He's been my best friend for as long as I can remember, but we grew even closer after his parents were killed by a drunk driver. He practically lived with my family from our sophomore year and on. We're closer than blood. I just hope that bond doesn't break with the choices I've made. I know they may be tested when he finds out about me and Kristen, but I pray that they don't break.

CHAPTER TWENTY-TWO

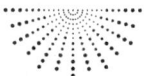

Kristen

It's Tuesday night, and I forgo seeing Derek because, hello? It's Taco and Tequila Tuesday. Mallory and Camryn are coming over for a girls' night, with pulled pork tacos, chips, salsa, and fresh guacamole. Yummy. I just finished making up some of my famous margarita mix and took the pork out of the oven. I hear a knock at the door and let the girls in. They're both subdued, which is very unlike them. Taking one look at their faces, I say, "Damn, it's going to be an extra margarita night tonight, isn't it?" They both nod their heads. "All right, ladies. Let's dish 'em up and chow down."

I start up a pitcher of margaritas and the girls help themselves to the tacos. I pour us all a big glass of the icy goodness and we head to the living room to eat. Camryn sits down on the carpet, and Mallory and I sit on the couch. "So, ladies, what's going on?"

Both of them answer in unison. "Man trouble."

"Well, hell. I didn't even know you were seeing anybody. When did this start?" Mallory and Camryn look at each other, trying to decide who's going to go first.

Camryn takes a big old drink of her margarita. "It's Isaac," she blurts out.

I look at her in shock. "What do you mean, Isaac? The band's Isaac?"

She nods her head. "We ran into each other a few months ago, when they were on break from their last tour. I don't know what the hell happened. It was about a month after Adam and I broke up, and I was feeling unwanted. I know he's a manwhore, but I slept with him anyway."

Holy shit! Camryn slept with Isaac? I can't wrap my head around that. Camryn's the good girl, the one who wants to be in a committed relationship before she'll have sex. One-night stand and Camryn do not go together. I take a drink of my margarita. "Okay. So, what happened?"

"I actually ran into him at Jake's bar. One of the girls I work with, her boyfriend, was playing that night, so a bunch of us went to show our support. He came over to the table, sat down, and we just talked. But the booze were flowing, and he's just so damn sexy. I don't know what the hell I was thinking. Some-how, we ended up back at his place." She blushes as she says it. "It may have only been one night, but damn, what a night. The only problem is he doesn't seem to want it to be just one night. He wants to date, exclusively. I don't know if he's capable of that, and I don't know if I want to risk my heart on a man like him."

"Yeah, that's a difficult decision, but Isaac is a nice guy, and he's honest. He's also upfront with the chicks he's with that he's a one-and-done. So, if he wants to date, maybe he's serious.

What would it hurt to go out with him a few times? Forget the exclusive for now. Just go have some fun, see where it takes you. You never know what can happen." She nods her head and finishes off her glass. She heads to the kitchen and brings the pitcher back, refills our glasses and sits it on the table in front of us.

She tips her glass to Mallory. "Your turn, girlfriend."

Mallory takes a long drink before she starts. "My problem is a little more complicated, I think. Y'all know I moved off with Todd not too long after my dad died." We both nod our heads. "I was a mess up there for a long time, but I finally started pulling myself together. Then things went sideways. Y'all don't know the real reason I moved back. I know I told you that it just didn't work out between us and I missed being home, which was true, but that wasn't the only reason. Todd..." She looks at us with tears in her eyes. "Todd was abusing me." Tears stream down her cheeks and she wipes them away from her face.

Mallory had moved from Texas a few months after we graduated, and met Todd the weekend after we graduated. He was almost too perfect, and I thought they moved way too fast. I felt that he pressured her to take the job in Colorado, especially since her dad had just died in a car accident. Before we even realized it, they packed up to move. Todd's family was from the area. For years, we only talked to her on the phone or on Facebook. Did we miss the warning signs? Now that I think back, there were some obvious red flags, but, as they say, hindsight is 20/20.

"My boss, Donna, had suspected what was going on and confronted me. She hounded me until I decided it was time to leave. I finally had enough. I made plans to move back here, and got everything set up. She even helped me get a job here, and got me an apartment in her name. She works with abuse victims in Colorado Springs, so she had a lot of contacts. I thought I had it all covered." She takes another drink of her margarita and finishes off her glass.

"Todd was supposed to be out of town with his brothers on a fishing trip. Donna had helped me pack up some stuff and had left to ship it. When she came back, she was taking me to the airport, but Todd got back before she did. It was bad. I can't talk much about it right now. Donna came back and found me, got me out. I don't remember a lot. She took me to the ER. They admitted me for a couple days, but I knew I needed to get away before he found me. They gave me enough pain meds to make it through the trip, and Donna ended up taking the plane with me. One of the docs she works with paid for her ticket and upgraded our seating so I would be more comfortable. We made it to Dallas and she took me to the apartment. She ended up staying with me for a while, to make sure there weren't any complications. I didn't realize the complex where I moved to was where Jason lived too, right next door. He saw me the night I came back, but he didn't realize it was me. I didn't even recognize me. Once Jason realized who I was a couple weeks later, he became protective of me, always checking in on me. He knew that I was scared. I told him what had happened, and he's been helping me deal with it all."

I have a hard time sitting here, letting her talk, but I'm afraid if I say anything, she won't tell us the rest. I just want to wrap her up and hold her tight. How could one of my best friends be going through this and not tell us?

"Anyway, Jason and I have gotten close, in a way. When they came back this weekend, he came over. I still don't believe it happened, but he kissed me. It's the first time I have kissed a man since Todd, and it was nice. Better than nice. It was getting a little intense and I freaked out when he put his hand in my hair." She sniffles. "Jason stopped as soon as he realized it and apologized. Then he left. I haven't heard from him since. I don't know if I can ever have a normal relationship again."

Camryn and I move around the table to her and hug her from each side. We all cry together. She needs to let this out. I pull back and rub the tears from her cheeks with my thumbs.

"Sweetie, of course you can have a normal relationship. It's just gonna take time, and patience on his part. But you need to be honest with him. Jason is a very complex man. He's the quiet one. He thinks things through before he acts, and that's probably what he's doing. And, if it's not, there are other guys out there."

"Now that we have this all out in the open, let's lighten up this sad girl's night," Mallory says as she wipes her face. "Who brought the chick flicks?"

"Wait. We haven't heard from Kristen yet. What's going on with you, girlfriend?"

Oh shit. What do I say? We decided to keep this quiet. If the girls are having some kind of relationship with the other guys... wait! These are my girls. They always have my back.

"Um, well...I am seeing someone. It's recent, but I've known him for years. I guess I finally decided that I needed to get back out there."

"I knew it. It's Josh, right? He never would let up with asking you out." Camryn chuckles.

"Well, I did have a date with Josh on Friday night, but it was a freaking disaster. He harped on what I was eating, and what diet he was on. He even slipped the waitress his phone number. I mean, really? Who does that shit. He even wanted a second date. Of course I said no, but he's a persistent bastard. He keeps texting me about going out again. He even cornered me at CrossFit the other morning. He just can't take no for an answer, says he can change my mind. What a douche."

"If it's not Josh, then who?"

"When I got home from my date, Derek came over."

"I thought the guys didn't come home until Saturday."

"Wait, Derek came over?"

They're asking the questions at the same time. I hold my hand up to get them to be quiet. If they get started, I'll never get to tell the story. "Derek flew home on Friday instead of riding the bus. He came over Friday afternoon. We just talked, and he even helped me pick out what I was going to wear on my date with Josh. After I got home, he knocked on the door, then he kissed me." I can feel my face heating up. "It just felt like it was meant to be."

I look at the girls and they're looking at me with their mouths hanging open. Camryn recovers first.

"Holy shit! Derek? Brett's best friend since diapers, Derek?" I nod my head.

"Well, when you decide to jump back on the relationship wagon, you do it big. Does Brett know?"

I shake my head. "Until now, no one knew. Well, except Jason. He saw us leaving Derek's place on Saturday afternoon. And now you two know. Please, keep this quiet. Our biggest concern is how Brett is going to take it. I thought he'd moved on. I mean, you see him all the time with different girls, but he showed up Saturday night. Derek was on his way over to take me out. I answered the door, expecting Derek, but it was Brett. He looked like hell. I was so uncomfortable. He told me he missed my voice, and the look in his eyes...it was so sad.

Neither of us want to hurt him, so we decided to keep it on the down low for a while. At least until Brett is a little more...stable, for lack of a better word. The guys were having a meeting about how to handle the situation. They had to confront Brett yesterday when he didn't show up at the studio."

"I'm still shocked that Derek is moving in on Brett's girl." I open my mouth to defend him, but Camryn continues. "I know you're not anymore, but doesn't it go against the 'bros before hoes' mentality? I mean, is he going to choose you over Brett if it comes down to it?"

She's voicing the same concerns I have. "I hope he doesn't have to choose. Brett and I have been over for a long time now. It's not like we just broke up."

"I know, but Brett broke your heart, and it took a long time to put those pieces back together. I just don't want to see it smashed to pieces again."

CHAPTER TWENTY-THREE

Derek

For the last two weeks, things have been going great. We have three more days before we leave for another four-month tour. All of us guys are here at the gym, getting our lift on. We've been here for about an hour longer than normal, and I'm almost ready to fall over. Brett and I are having a contest to see who can do the most pull-ups. I'm going to win, of course, because Brett is still recovering from his, shall we say, overindulgence in pussy, alcohol, and drugs. He's been doing well, staying with Brian, and Brian has been keeping track of everything that Brett does. I think Brian may even be monitoring how many times he shits or spends time with his right hand. Brett has put some of the weight back on that he's lost, with Brian's housekeeper keeping him well-fed.

We keep going—up, down, up, down—and I can tell that he's tiring out. We go up one more time and he's done. I drop right after he does.

"Damn, what a work out. I'm ready for a shower and some food. How ya feeling, Brett?" I look over and see him bent at the waist, huffing in air, but he gives me a thumbs up. I grab a couple bottles of water and toss him one. "Drink up, man. You still gotta drink one of those protein shakes too." He grimaces as he guzzles the water, then we head off to the showers. Jason and Isaac holler at us that they're almost finished and will catch up with us. We get cleaned up and get dressed.

We all load up into Isaacs's SUV and head to the studio. We've made a lot of progress on the new album, and this may be our best album yet. We've laid down most of the tracks and we have to get Brett working on vocals. Since he's gotten more focused, his heart is back in the band.

I've gotten to spend a lot of time with Kristen too. We haven't spent many nights apart, except for a couple of girls' nights. I can't help but feel like I walk around with a stupid grin on my face every time I think of her. I feel more comfortable with her than any other girl I've been with in a relationship. Not that there are that many—three total. I think it's because I've known her so long as a friend. I think it's one of the things that will make us last.

"What's got you grinning like that?" I look over at Brett and wipe the smile off my face. "Nothing, really. Just thinking how well we've all been doing these last couple weeks. This album is going to rock. I think this may just be our best album yet. I'm excited to get this tour done so we can take a long break because I'm afraid we're going to burn out if we keep going at this pace. I love you guys, but sometimes I'd like to wake up and y'all not be the first thing I see." I give a small chuckle and hope I have diverted his curiosity.

Now he has a questioning look on his face. "Well, I agree

with you on the album. It's gonna be epic. But for some reason, I don't think that's the reason for the grin." He looks away. Well, fuck. I really don't want to go down this road right now. Luckily, we pull into Brian's and head to the studio. We go inside and Brian and the producer are looking at something on the computer. Brian looks up when we enter.

"Morning, guys. Y'all ready for a long day?" We all groan, and he laughs. "Too bad. We're on a roll and I want to get as much done as we can before we leave. We don't want to lose any momentum. Brett, I need you to work on the vocals for Somewhere. Derek, it's time for you to work on the bass line for From Now On. We also have three more songs that we need to try and get done before we leave on Wednesday. The feedback that I'm getting from the recording company is great so far."

We all head to our respective rooms, and Jason comes with me. Sometimes, I can work better with the two of us in the room. We can play off each other and the results are amazing. I'm still shocked with how well some of the tracks have turned out. We have really poured our hearts and souls into this album.

We leave in a few days for another jam-packed tour that will give us little time off. I hate that we're going to be on the bus that long, and I hate that I'm going to be away from Kristen for even a night. I'm also concerned with how me being gone on tour will affect her. Last time her boyfriend went on tour, he cheated on her. I know that will never happen with me, but I'm sure that she thought the same thing about Brett.

WE WORKED LATE TONIGHT. I'd told Kristen that we would probably work late since we only have a few days to go. I texted her to make sure she was still up for me coming over, and if she wanted me to bring something to eat. She responded back that she had made dinner, and there was plenty left over for me. Kristen is a great cook, and she has really spoiled me the last couple weeks. At first, I worried that I was putting her out by her cooking, but she insists that she loves it. She doesn't cook a whole lot since she lives alone, so when she does , she eats left-overs for a week. Since I eat so much, she's able to cook more without it going to waste.

I stop by my house on the way to grab some clean clothes for the next few days. I want to spend all the time I can with her.

I pull up into her parking lot and see a truck that looks familiar. It belongs to that douchebag she went on a date with. I pass the truck on the way to her door and notice that it's empty. I knock on Kris' door. When there's no answer, I start to get a bad feeling. I twist the knob and the door opens. I can hear the shower running from her open bedroom door. I head that way to let her know that I'm here so it won't scare her if she hears me moving around. I clear the doorway and see that fucker laid out on her bed, naked. What. The. Fuck! He sees me standing there and tries to cover up with the blanket that Kris leaves on the end of the bed.

"What the fuck are you doing in here?" I ask him as he scrambles around. I start to move toward him and hear Kris yell out, "Babe, you here? I left you a plate in the fridge if you want to heat it up. I'll be out in a minute."

I know that Kris isn't a cheater, but my heart feels a little bit lighter when she calls out to me.

"Kris, you stay in there for a minute. I think you have an unwanted visitor in here."

"What?" I can hear her scrambling around in the bathroom.

"Make sure you put some clothes on if you're coming out here. That douche you went out with a couple weeks ago is naked on your bed."

I see the door swing open and she steps out in a T-shirt and shorts. She just stares at the guy on her bed. "Josh, what the fuck are you doing in my apartment?"

I look back to Josh, who's standing beside the bed with the blanket wrapped around his waist, and he's blushing.

"I just wanted to surprise you, and convince you we would be good together. I didn't realize you were, um...seeing someone else."

"How the fuck did you get in here, you motherfucker? I ought to call the cops right now. What kind of sick fuck comes in to a woman's home and gets naked so she can find him? It's not like you have a relationship with her! She went out with you once, and from what she said, it did not go well. You even gave the waitress your phone number. I mean, what kind of man does that?"

I'm getting louder with every question I ask him. I've even started moving toward him, but Kristen stops me from moving by stepping in-between us and putting her hand on my chest to stop my advance.

Josh is trying to pick up his clothes off the floor while keeping his eyes on me. "The door was open. I knocked, but she didn't answer. I opened the door and hollered for her, but didn't hear anything. Then I heard the shower running and decided to surprise her. I guess it was stupid, now that I think about it."

I whisper to Kris to go in the living room and call the cops. If I hadn't shown up, who knows what would have happened.

She nods her head and heads that way. I stay in the bedroom. "Look, motherfucker, if I find out you've come anywhere near her again, you will not like what happens. Stay right where the fuck you are. She's calling the cops right now." He looks at me with a panicked expression.

"We don't need to involve the cops, do we? Come on, I just made a mistake. My bad. I can just get out of here. No harm, no foul."

"No harm, huh? What the fuck was your plan when she came out of that shower, huh? No rational person would do something like this without some evil fucking thoughts in his head."

I hear someone knock on the door and Kris goes to answer it. I can hear her talking to someone and she walks in with a cop. I recognize him from seeing him around the complex. "Man, you got here quick," I say, shaking his hand.

"Denny was coming back home to grab some food when he heard the call go out. He was already in the parking lot."

"Glad to be of service. So, what's going on?"

I explain what I found when I got here. When I finish, he gets to asking Josh questions. He allows Josh to put his pants back on before he cuffs him and heads out the door. Kris had snuck out of the room at some point and has made some supper for Denny, since his was interrupted. We watch him put Josh in the back of his cruiser, then he walks back over to us.

"Denny, I'm really glad that you were close. Thank you. I packed you some supper since you didn't get yours." Kris hands him over a Tupperware container."

"Thanks, Kris. Look, make sure you press charges on this guy. It won't be a big charge, since he didn't actually do any breaking and entering. And it'll be a he said/she said situation.

Just don't get your hopes up that he'll actually go to jail. He'll probably just get a fine."

Kris nods her head. "I just want him out of here. It's freaking creepy. I only had the door unlocked because Derek was coming over and I needed to shower. I'll never do that again, I promise."

"Kris, head back in the house, babe." She nods her head and goes back in.

I turn to Denny. "I don't like this man. No normal person does this kind of shit. What would have happened if I hadn't shown up? The thought scares the shit out of me. Can you keep an eye on her? I leave for my next tour on Wednesday, and I'll be gone for four months. If he's not going to jail, I'd feel better with another pair of eyes on her."

"Of course. It's not a problem. This is part of my regular patrol, and I only live a couple apartments down. Has she ever done any type of self-defense?" I shake my head no. "I have a friend who teaches Krav Maga, specifically for women. It probably wouldn't hurt for her to do that. Maybe better locks on the doors. An alarm system could help. It'll help you keep your peace of mind too." He gets a card out of his wallet and gives it to me for his friend. I thank him again and head inside.

I see Kris sitting on the couch with her head buried in her hands. I crouch down in front of her and put my hands on the sides of her face, forcing her to look up at me. I see the tears sliding down her cheeks, and I wipe them away with my thumbs. "You're okay, baby. He's gone."

"I just feel so stupid for leaving my door unlocked. What if you hadn't shown up? It's scary. I never would have expected this from him."

I gather her up in my arms and hug her to me. We just sit

there as I comfort her. Finally, she pulls away and stands up. "Guess I can go heat up your supper." She tries to give me a smile before she heads into the kitchen. I have to give myself a minute to gather myself. I can't show her how much this freaked me out, especially after talking with Denny. I head into the kitchen and walk up behind her. I wrap my arms around her stomach and pull her back against me. I just need to hold her.

CHAPTER TWENTY-FOUR

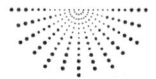

Kristen

I walk back into the apartment, leaving Derek outside with Denny. I feel so freaking stupid. I know better than to leave my freaking door unlocked. What if Derek hadn't come when he did? I sit on the couch and bury my face in my hands.

I hear Derek come back in, but I can't look at him. He crouches down in front of me and wipes the tears from my cheeks, trying to comfort me. I head to the kitchen to heat up his supper when I feel him move in behind me and draw me to him. He kisses the right side of my neck.

God, how is it that he can turn me on with just a touch? I'm already wet. He takes his left hand and roughly grabs the hair on the top of my head, giving him better access to my neck. With his free hand, he rips my shirt from chest to waist and grabs my breast, squeezing it hard. I don't think I've ever been so turned on in my life. I can feel my juices running down my thighs. He lets go of my hair and runs his hand down my torso, down my stomach and into my shorts. I didn't put on panties earlier so he has easy access to my pussy. He runs his fingers between my lips, and when he feels how wet I am, he groans against my skin.

"Fuck, baby. I need you so bad. Lean down and put your hands on the counter." I lean back and he pulls what's left of my shirt and shorts past my hips and they pool at my feet. I step out of them and he spreads my legs apart with his leg. He starts to place kisses and bites down my back as he makes his way down to my ass. Moving my cheeks slightly apart, I feel his tongue lick me from my opening to my clit in slow sweeps.

"You taste so fucking good. I could eat you all day long." He sticks his tongue into my opening and swirls it around, then moves back down to my clit and flicks it with his tongue, while pushing his fingers into me. He goes rough and hard. Before I realize it, my orgasm sweeps through me. I feel like I'm going to black out. Before my legs start to give way, he stands and thrusts his big dick into me with one hard thrust. I can feel myself clenching around him as he pounds away at me. Grabbing me by my hair, he pulls my head back, making my body arch.

"Come on my cock, Kris. Give it to me." With a few more hard, deep thrusts, I clench around him again and cry out. "Fuuuck, yes!" He thrusts twice more and stiffens.

"I love you, Kris."

"I love you, too."

He reaches down and kisses me, slowly. "God, baby. What did I do to deserve you?" He helps me stand and picks me up, bridal style, and tries to carry me to the bedroom without his pants falling down. It's so funny, and I try not to laugh. By the time we make it to the bedroom, his pants have made it all the way down and he's laughing with me. He tosses me on the bed and sits down to take off his clothes. He took me fully dressed.

I roll off the bed and go into the bathroom to clean up, which reminds me to check and see when my next shot is due. I head back to the bedroom and find him sprawled out on the bed. When he sees me, he moves the covers back for me to crawl in bedside him. I cuddle up next to him and lay my head on his chest, my hand on his abs.

"Tonight scared the hell out of me, Kris. I want you to think about taking a self-defense class. Denny gave me a card for his friend that teaches Krav Maga for women." He runs his hand up and down my back. "I'm going to get you an alarm system." Before I can say anything, he continues. "It's for my peace of mind, as well as your safety. And maybe see about getting you a better lock. Denny suggested that too."

"If it will make you feel better, okay. And I'll see about the self-defense class. I may see if Camryn and Mallory want to take it too." I take my finger and trace it through the muscles on his stomach, to the V at his pelvis. My hand tangles in the hair around his dick, then I retrace my steps back up. Back down. Every time I get near his dick, he tenses up and twitches beneath the covers.

Kissing his chest, I wrap my hand around his dick, slowly stroking him up and down. I move my lips across his chest, down his stomach, and down to where I am holding him tight. I move the covers back and situate myself between his legs. Running my thumb across the tip, I gather the wetness and look up to see him watching me with hooded eyes. I lick my lips, then run my tongue around the head like an ice cream cone. He tastes musky, salty. I move my hand lower, toward the base, and close my lips over the tip. I make a few shallow passes and he groans. Encouraged, I take him slightly deeper with each pass, moving my hand up and down as I take as much of him into my mouth as I can. He's too big for me to take all of him, but I do my damnedest to swallow as much as I can. I move my other hand down to squeeze his balls, then roll them around in my hand. He moves his hands to my head and gently thrusts his hips toward my face, a little quicker each time, going a little deeper. I move one finger to the skin behind his balls and he groans. "Enough."

Reaching down, he grabs me under my arms and drags me up his body so I'm straddling him. Grabbing me by my hips, he shoves me down onto his cock as he pulls us together, chest to chest. He kisses me hard, thrusting his tongue in my mouth like he can't get enough of me. He makes tiny little thrusts with his hips before laying back down on the pillows.

"Ride me, Kris."

I begin to slowly raise and lower myself over him, savoring the feel of him splitting me wide. He moves his hands to my hips and starts to control the speed. It feels so good. He begins to thrust his hips up harder, so I move my hands back and place them on his thighs to change the angle. He moves one hand to my clit, and the other to my breast. When he adds pressure to my clit and pinches my nipple, I fall apart.

My orgasm is still washing through me when he flips us over and places my ankles over his shoulders. He pounds into me, hitting my G-spot with each thrust. God, I can feel myself building again. He lifts me a little higher and it changes the position just enough to set me off with the next thrust.

"That's it, baby. Come for me. Let me feel your tight little pussy grip around me." He shoves my legs over my shoulders and continues to pound into me. He thrusts a few more times before he stiffens against me. As he comes, he slows his pace and watches as he moves in and out of me. It's hot as hell. Finally, he pulls out of me, breathing hard.

"I think I can miss my work out tomorrow." I grin at him and he smiles. Rolling off of me, he pulls me close to him.

"I meant what I said, Kris. I love you. I don't know exactly when it happened, but I can't deny it anymore."

"And I meant it when I said it back."

"I've been thinking a lot lately, about the band and us going on tour. I don't want you to worry when I go. I don't want you to stress over it. When we get back, we're going to take a long break. I'm tired of being on the road all the time."

I think about what he's saying. It hasn't even crossed my mind that he would cheat on me, and I tell him as much. He leans down and kisses me softly.

"Good. I never want you to lose faith in me. These four months will fly by. When I get back, I think we should let everyone know about us. I think Brett is on a good path right now, but this tour is going to put that to the test. Are you okay with waiting that long?"

I nod my head and kiss his chest. "I can wait that long. It won't change how we feel. I want Brett to be in a good place. I want him to eventually find his happiness."

"All right, baby. Let's get some sleep. It's been a long day." He switches off the light and I snuggle in. It doesn't take me long before I sink into sleep with the feel of his hand rubbing my back.

CHAPTER TWENTY-FIVE

Kristen

Derek and the guys have been gone for a couple months now. I'm really missing him, even though we talk often on the phone and Skype when his schedule allows. It's nice to know that he misses me as much as I miss him. It's also sweet how he keeps sending me flowers to my home and office, along with cards. Today he sent some chocolates—yummy, delicious chocolates. I'm going to have to kick his ass when he gets home because I'll have to work out extra to keep from gaining more weight. Mallory, Camryn, and I started taking the self-defense class that Denny recommended. I was so happy that Mallory agreed to it because I was worried about her. We were also able to talk her into seeing a psychologist. She needed to talk to someone to help her understand she could have a "normal" relationship. We all find the self-defense class fun, and I feel a lot stronger, safer. Like I can kick ass if I need to.

Josh had gotten released the morning after Denny arrested

him. They said they really couldn't charge him with anything more than a misdemeanor. They couldn't get a restraining order either, since there was no prior contact of this type, and he didn't have any record showing a history of assault. That's scary to me. I'm glad Derek suggested getting the alarm system. I found out that Josh was also fired, so since he was no longer at our box, I started doing CrossFit again. The guy has been seriously creeping me out. He's still texting me, even though he was warned by Denny to stop. I would swear that I've seen him outside my work, and when I've been out at the store. Nothing says creeper more than trying to spy on a woman when she's underwear shopping.

It's Monday, and work has been busy, as usual, with lots of sick kids and stressed out parents. I've been puked on, peed on, and snotted on. But it's all in the line of duty. All I can think of when I pull into the parking lot at my apartment complex is taking a long, hot shower. When I walk up to my door, I find an envelope with a rose lying in front of my door. Thinking it's another card from Derek, I smile, pick it up and unlock the door. Once I'm inside, I lock it back and set the alarm.

Walking into my bedroom, I throw my purse and card on the bed before making my way to the bathroom for a very hot shower.

When I finish, I throw on my 'around the house' clothes and grab the envelope . Opening it, I find pictures of me in my living room, in my car, and out shopping. Hell, there's even some of me at work. What the fuck? When I get to the last photo, I find a note.

YOU'RE MINE. Don't forget.

. . .

WELL, if that didn't scare the shit out of someone, I don't know what would. I drop the note and pictures on my bed, like they're going to bite me. Shit, what do I do? I immediately call Denny to see if he has any suggestions. I'm glad he gave Derek his number so I could call him.

"Hello?"

"Denny? It's Kristen. I'm sorry to call you, but I'm really scared. I found an envelope and a rose on my doorstep when I got home from work today. They're a bunch of pictures of me at home and at work. Is there any way you can drop by and check it out?"

"Yeah, I'm right around the block. Don't touch it any more than you already have. Is your door locked? Alarm set?"

"Yes."

"Keep it that way until I get there."

I sit on the couch until I hear a knock at the door. I check to make sure it's Denny before I undo the alarm and disengage the locks.

"Where is it?"

"As soon as I saw what was in it, I dropped it and left it on the bed."

"Is this the first time?"

"First time for what?"

"That you received an envelope? Have you received anything else out of the ordinary?"

"I don't think so." But I get to thinking. None of the flowers that I've been receiving have had Derek's name on them.

"I've been getting flowers at work and at home. I figured

they were from Derek, but thinking back, they've never had his name on them."

"How do you know they're not? Didn't he mention them? Didn't you thank him?"

"Jeez, what kind of freaking girlfriend am I? An unappreciative one, apparently. I haven't even thanked him for them. We don't get to talk but a few times a week, and I'm just happy to hear from him, ya know?

"I'll check into it. Do you know what florist delivered them?"

"Hang on a second, I've kept all the cards. They're in the bedroom too."

I head back to my room and Denny follows me. I point out the pictures and the letter that are lying on the bed before I move to my dresser and open my keepsake box. I begin to go through them, finding that they're each from different florists. I hand them over to Denny.

"I'm gonna call one of my friends on the force, a detective. Maybe he can open a case. I have to tell you, though, there's not a whole lot we can do with pictures, a letter, and flowers."

Denny pulls out his cell phone and makes the call. He doesn't touch anything else and lays the cards on the bed out. We walk out to the living room and I head to the kitchen to make some coffee while we wait. About fifteen minutes later, there's another knock at the door. Denny answers it and lets in an older gentleman.

"This is Detective Reinhardt. I've explained to him what's going on, but you're gonna need to repeat what you've told me. I think you need to start at the Josh incident."

Detective Reinhardt takes a seat across from me, and I do as Denny suggests. After I'm finished, Detective Reinhardt speaks.

"I think you may have a stalker, which puts us in a precarious position. What he's done hasn't broken the law, no matter how uncomfortable it makes you feel. Did you get the restraining order?"

I shake my head no. "There wasn't enough evidence to grant one."

"Well, that makes it even more difficult. What you need to do is be very vigilant and cautious of your surroundings. Do not go anywhere alone. I'm going to look further into this Josh guy, see what kind of background I can pull up on him. But, for now, that's really all we can do." He stands up and shakes my hand. "You be careful, my dear."

Denny stays for a few more minutes, but he has to get back to work. Before he leaves, he tells me to let Derek know what's going on. Once he leaves, I turn on the TV and try to take my mind off of things. If Derek calls me, it won't be until later. But, since it's a work night, he may not call at all. He tries to be considerate, knowing I have to get up in the morning for work. I can't decide if I'm going to tell him about this right now or not. There's not a lot he can do when he's a thousand miles away. I'll take the detective's advice to be vigilant, and always stick with other people. I know Camryn and Mallory won't have a problem with me dragging them along to go shopping.

I finally find myself dozing off and head to bed. Luckily, the detective took all the pictures and letters and things with him since he needed them as evidence. I double check to make sure the doors are locked and the alarm is set. I even check the windows to make sure they're locked.

I sleep pretty fretfully, and I'm dragging ass the next morning. CrossFit is out because there's no way I'll be able to do it this morning. Instead, I get ready for work. As I'm leaving, I notice a piece of paper stuck under the door. I don't want to pick it up, but I do.

Don't think they can protect you. You're mine.

Well, fuck.

I'M on my way to work when Derek calls. I hit the button on my steering wheel to answer the phone and hear his voice through my speakers.

"Hey, baby, how are you this morning?" His sleep roughened voice makes my girly parts take notice.

"I didn't sleep too well last night, but it's nice to hear your voice this morning. What are you doing, calling me this early?"

"I woke up and needed to hear your voice since I didn't get to talk to you last night. Our show ran pretty late. How was work?"

I tell him about the Monday from hell, then ask him about the flowers. It's not what I wanted to hear.

"I wish I had thought about it, babe, but no, I haven't sent you any flowers. What's going on?"

I tell him about getting the flowers at work and home, so I just assumed they were from him. "I found an envelope and a rose on my doorstep after work yesterday. I called Denny, and he called a detective about it, but as of right now, there's nothing they can do."

"Fuck, Kristen. I wish I was home right now. Are you doing okay?"

I tell him about the advice I got from the detective, and that I'm just going to be really careful. I don't know what else to do. I can't stop living my life, wondering what's going to happen next.

"Two more months and I'll be home. I bet it's that damn Josh guy. I knew there was something fucking creepy about him. If you see him anywhere, let Denny know. I feel so fucking help-less right now."

"Don't feel that way. There's nothing any of us can do at this point. I'm making sure to set my alarm and lock all the doors and windows. I'm taking the self-defense class with the girls, and I'll do my best to not go anywhere by myself. I'll let Denny know if I see him." I don't tell him about the note under the door this morning. I think the information I've given him already is enough for now.

We talk for a few more minutes before saying our goodbyes, and then I call Denny. I let him know about the note I found this morning. He promises to go by my apartment sometime today to fingerprint the door. But, in the meantime, there's nothing else they can do.

CHAPTER TWENTY-SIX

Derek

I can't wait for this fucking tour to be over. We've been gone for three months, but it feels like an eternity. I can't keep my mind off Kristen and what she's going through on her own. That fucker keeps sending her flowers to her work and home. More chocolates. He even started sending her jewelry. They can't trace anything back to that fucker, though.

I feel so fucking useless this far away from her. The cops haven't been able to track down Josh; it's like he's vanished into thin air. I called a private investigator to see if he could find anything that the cops had overlooked. He was able to discover that another PI was hired to take pictures of her, but he wasn't able to disclose who had paid him, though. He's stopped leaving notes at her door, and now leaves them on her car. I've talked to Denny regularly, and I know he's patrolling around the area as much as he can. I just find it hard to believe that no one can remember seeing Josh anywhere around the apartment complex. I mean, it's hard to miss the guy. He doesn't exactly blend in to the normal crowd built the way he is. To top off this whole fucked up situation, my ex cheating bitch somehow got ahold of my cell phone number. I'd changed it after we broke up because she wouldn't leave me alone. When I realized it was her, I hung up on her and blocked her number. But that hasn't stopped her from leaving me a shit ton of messages. I have no fucking clue how she even got my number, or why she's even bothering after all this time.

It's almost time for us to go on, and my phone vibrates in my pocket. I grab it and see it's from Kristen. It's not her normal 'knock 'em dead' or 'rock out.' It's 'Call me as soon as your show is over.' What. The. Fuck! I move to call her right then, but Brett walks over to me with the other guys. The opening band has finished and it's our turn to take the stage. Fuck, I can't delay the show. I'll call her as soon as I can, after the show.

We play our opening number, and I'm playing the chords with no feeling. My heart just isn't in it tonight. I think that Brett can tell because he keeps shooting glances my way. We're supposed to play one of our new songs tonight, one we just finished recording, but for the life of me, I can't remember the chords. I signal for Brett to take five before I start the opening of Somewhere. He gives Isaac a look and he goes into a guitar solo to give us some time.

"What the fuck is up with you tonight, man?"

"Sorry. I just can't get my head in the game tonight. Can we skip Somewhere? For the life of me, I can't remember my chords."

"Okay, man, we'll skip it for tonight. Brian isn't gonna be happy about it, but we'll work it out."

He walks away from me to go tell Jason and Isaac the change in plans. Jason looks over at me with a questioning look, and I shrug my shoulders. Jason knows that Kristen has a stalker, but he's the only one.

We finish out the night with our usual songs. The crowd is into it, and Brett is rocking the hell out of this show. We all do our little solos when he introduces us to the crowd. Mine's a little shorter than usual. I usually grab the guitar I keep by me and do some solo work on it, but I can't get Kristen's message out of my head. What the hell is going on?

We wrap up the show after two encores, and Brian meets us at the side. I can't tell if he's mad or not. I'm the first one off the stage and he grabs my arm as I hurry by. Whatever he sees in my face has him letting me go. I can hear Jason calling my name as I run down the corridor. I go into the first empty room that I find, with Jason hot on my heels. He closes the door as I pull my phone out and dial her number. She can't answer it fast enough for me, but it goes to voicemail. "Fuck!" As soon as the scream leaves my mouth, my phone vibrates in my hand. It's her.

"Kris, baby, what's going on?" As soon as she hears my voice, she starts to sob, then someone else comes on the line.

"Derek? It's Mallory."

"Jesus, Mal. What the fuck is going on? Is Kris okay?"

"Oh, God. She's fine, physically. When she came home from work today, there was a dead kitten on her stoop. It had…" I can hear her take a deep breath, then her voice cracks. "It had been gutted. It was bad. She's been a wreck ever since she found it."

I can feel myself sink to my knees. Just knowing that she's

physically okay makes me weak with relief, and Jason places a hand on my shoulder. Jason takes the phone from me and talks to Mallory as he moves away from me. I can hear him talking, but I can't make out the words. After what seems like an eternity, Jason walks back to me and hands me the phone.

"I'll tell you everything Mallory told me as soon as you finish talking to Kristen. Be supportive. That's what she needs right now."

As he walks out the door, leaving me alone, I place the phone back to my ear and hear Mallory tell Kris I'm on the phone again.

"Derek, I'm scared." And with those two words, she rips my heart out. I feel so fucking useless. I'm hundreds of miles away from her and I can't physically comfort or protect her.

"Oh, baby. I'm sorry I'm not there right now. I just want to wrap you up in my arms. I'm going to see if we can cut this tour short, or maybe find someone to take my place for the rest of it. I need to be with you right now. I love you."

"I love you too, but you can't come home right now. You only have a month left, and then you'll be home. This just freaked me out. I called Denny and he came over and took care of it. Mallory came and picked me up and I'm going to stay with her tonight."

I hear the door open and see Jason stick his head in, giving me the signal to wrap it up. I forgot we have an interview with the magazine tonight.

"Babe, I have to go. We have that interview tonight. Fuck! I just want to be with you. I'm sorry all this is happening, and I'm pissed that I can't be there to fix this right now. I love you so much, more than you'll ever know." I can hear her quietly sobbing in the background.

"I love you too, more than I ever thought possible. I know you would be here if you could, but I'm counting down the days until you're here with me." We talk for a few more minutes and say our goodbyes. Jason walks in the door.

"We have to go to that interview. Is your head on straight now?"

"As straight as it's going to be with all this shit going on. I feel like the most worthless person in the fucking world. My girl needs me and I can't be there for her. What if something happens to her before we get back? I'll never forgive myself if I could have prevented her from being hurt."

"This isn't your fault, and you couldn't have stopped this from happening. Yeah, it sucks that you're here and she's there right now. I know how it feels." I quirk an eyebrow at him, silently asking the question. "Not now, man. Later, I'll tell you all about it. Right now, we have to go do this interview before Brian has a coronary."

We walk out the door and see Brian, Brett, and Isaac waiting for us. They all have questioning looks on their faces, but I don't know what to tell them. "Sorry. Small panic back home, but I think it's taken care of for now. That may change at any time, though."

"Derek, are your parents okay?" Brett has a worried look on his face. He loves my parents. They were really there for him after his parents died, and they treated him like one of their own.

"Yeah. They're fine, Brett."

"Okay, boys, let's get y'all interviewed so we can call it a night." Brian practically herds us to another room that's already set up. There's a beautiful brunette sitting in the room. I know I'm taken, but this chick is banging, and she's eyeing all of us. I feel a tad bit uncomfortable, and I hope it doesn't show.

"Well, hello, boys," she purrs, and I just want to roll my eyes. I look at the others, and Brett is the only one paying attention to her. He goes and stands beside her, while the rest of us move to the chairs that are out. This is interesting. Normally, Isaac and Brett would be fighting for the hottie's attention. As her and Brett speak, she runs a nail down his arm as she looks over at me, giving me a wink. Oh, she's one of those. A newer reporter to the magazine, wanting a big interview with some behind-the-scenes to sell. Build up her rep. Well, sorry darlin', you won't be getting anything from me. I shake my head at her and look away. Brian finally takes control so we can get this over with.

She asks the typical questions. How did you start out? At Jake's Bar. Who discovered you? Brian. Where do you see the band in five years? Hopefully, still making music and loving it. How about women? Brett, weren't you in a serious relationship for a long time and got engaged? What happened there?

The question of Brett and Kristen has come up before, and Brett never really handled the question well. I'm hoping he doesn't blow up now.

"I fucked up and it ended. End of story." Wow. I was not expecting him to remain calm when he answered. Maybe he's finally coming to grips with them not being together.

"So, what about the rest of you gentlemen? I know you guys don't lack for female attention. What does it take to keep you at attention? I mean, your attention?" She licks her lips as she eyes Isaac, then bends forward slightly to show us more of her cleavage. Before Kristen, I would have been all over this chick. Now? I just see her as pathetic.

"Nothing you have, sweetheart. Any other questions for us tonight? We're sweaty, tired, hungry, and thirsty." I stand and walk out, with Jason and Isaac right behind me. Brett can get his fill and appease her. That's fine with me. I know what I have waiting at home. She's the best part of me.

CHAPTER TWENTY-SEVEN

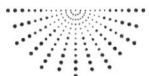

Kristen

One more week. Just one more week until Derek gets home. I'm so ready to see him, hug him, smell him. I'm horny as hell, but I'm also tired. I haven't had a decent night's sleep since the cat incident. I stayed a few nights at Mallory's after it happened, but eventually, I had to come home. I wake at every little noise. The flower deliveries have all but stopped, and I don't know whether to be relieved or worried. I've pretty much limited myself to home, work, CrossFit, and self-defense class. I've limited my grocery shopping to once a week. I'm used to going out a few times a week with the girls, so I hate having this fear.

It's was a late night at work. One night a week we have a night clinic, and it was my turn to work. I'm halfway to my car when I realize how dark it is. I look up to find that half the lights in the parking lot are out. I feel the hairs on the back of my neck stand up, feeling like someone is watching me. I walk faster and grab my keys out of my purse so I can hit the panic button if I need to. I think I can hear footsteps behind me, but I don't want to look back. Suddenly, I feel a tug on my purse that jerks me back, and I push the button. When the alarm goes off, the pressure releases and I hear the person running away. I run to my car, get in and lock the doors. I'm breathing so hard, I'm afraid I'm going to hyperventilate. I grab my phone to call Derek, but what can he do right now? He'll be my second call. I call Denny and tell him what's happened. His first piece of advice is to leave the parking lot. I start the car and head out, looking in my rearview mirror every few seconds. I don't see anyone, and when I turn onto the main road, I breathe out a sigh of relief. Denny tells me to head home and he'll meet me there.

I probably drive way too fast on the way home. Once I make it to my apartment, I run inside, lock the door and set the alarm. I text Denny to let him know I made it home. I go to call Derek, but remember he's in the middle of a concert some-where in Kansas. I send him a text instead that I hope he has a kick ass night and that I want him to call me after, no matter what time he's done. I can't sit still. I guess my adrenaline is still flowing. I hear a knock at the door, and I check the peep hole to see that it's Denny, but he's not in uniform. I turn off the alarm and disengage the locks to let him in.

"Oh my gosh, Denny. I wasn't even thinking that you may have been off work. I'm so sorry."

"It's okay, Kristen. I was just hanging out with the guys, watching the game. I'm glad you called. Now, tell me what happened."

I tell him what happened when I left work. "I don't know if someone was just trying to mug me or if it was him. I never even saw the person. I just heard the footsteps coming toward me, and when I felt the tug on my purse, I pushed the panic button on my car and they ran away. That's when I got in the car and called you."

"Okay. Your office is in Crawford Plaza?" I nod my head. "I'll head over there tomorrow and see if they have any surveillance video from the parking lot, and speak to whoever manages the Plaza to get those lights fixed. To tell you the truth, I don't know if it's related to your stalker, or if it was some punk just looking for a quick buck. Have you thought about getting your license to carry?"

"I've never shot a gun."

"That's okay. I can take you to a range and teach you how to shoot. Then you can take the class and get your permit. Unless you have something on your record I don't know about?" He smiles at me.

"Not unless speeding tickets count."

"No, I think you're good. I'm off Saturday morning, we can go then." I nod my head, knowing that I don't have anything planned.

"Just wear some comfortable clothes, and I'll bring everything else that we'll need."

We head to the door and he turns to me. He grabs me in a loose hug and kisses the top of my head. Well, this is a little awkward.

"I'm not going to let anything happen to you, Kris. When does Derek come back?"

"Next week, on Thursday."

"Good. I know you'll feel better when he's home. We'll get some lunch on Saturday too, if that's okay with you?"

"That should be fine."

He opens the door and walks out. I lock it and set the alarm.

I can tell my adrenaline is gone because I can feel myself fading fast. I head to the kitchen and make a quick sandwich for supper, then sit on the couch and turn on Ink Master. I must have dozed off because my phone ringing startles me awake. I quickly grab the phone and see that it's Derek.

"Hey, Derek."

"Hey, babe. How's your night?"

I tell him about what happened after work, and about Denny offering to take me shooting this weekend. I also tell him that if it goes well, I may get my license to carry permit.

"If you get comfortable enough shooting, I think that's a great idea. When I get back, I'll get mine too. I won't always be able to carry mine since the law differs from state to state. If it will give you a sense of security, I'm all for it."

"I'm glad. Listen, I'm fading fast, Derek. I can hardly keep my eyes open. I love you, and I'm so ready for you to be home next week."

"I love you too. Get some sleep. Hopefully, Thursday will be here before we know it. I miss holding you at night."

We hang up and I feel a little bit better being able to hear his voice before I go to sleep. I gather up my dishes and put them in the dishwasher, turn off the TV and head into bathroom to do my nightly routine for my skin. I change into one of Derek's shirts to sleep in, climb into bed, and I'm out before my head hits the pillow.

SOMETHING JOLTS ME AWAKE. It takes me a second to realize that someone's car alarm is going off. I look at the clock, and it's three in the morning. Motherfucker. I jump up and grab a pair of yoga pants. The closer I get to my living room, the louder the alarm is. I glance out the peep hole and see a shadow, then a loud knock on my door. I let out a scream because it scares the crap out of me.

"Kris? It's me, Denny. Your car alarm is going off. Can you silence it?"

I turn around and grab the keys off the table and hit the button to turn off the alarm before I head back to the door. I slip on a pair of flip flops and fling the door open.

"What happened?" He points to my car, and I see that someone has thrown something at the windshield. It's shattered, and there's a knife sticking out of my front tire. Holy shit.

"I've already called someone from the department to come out. I'll let you know when they get here. Why don't you go back in until they get here? Nothing like the whole complex looking out their windows at you. I'll head to the manager's office in a few hours and check the surveillance tapes, and I'll also let Detective Reinhardt know what happened so he can add it to your file."

"Th—Thanks, Denny," I stutter out as my body shakes. I'm so scared. I guess he can tell because he hugs me.

He lets me go and walks me into the apartment. I head to the kitchen to make coffee because there's no way I'm going back to sleep after this. After Denny leaves to get ready for work, I take my coffee and sit on the couch. I turn on the TV, just to have some noise to drown out the silence, and text my boss, letting her know what happened last night and just now. Then I inform her that I won't be in. Next, I text Camryn to let her know I won't be at CrossFit. Last, I text Derek, asking him to call me when he wakes up.

As soon as eight a.m. rolls around, I call the insurance company to see about getting a rental car. Denny said they would probably take my car for evidence. They ask me to take pictures to send them before it gets taken to the impound lot, so I head out to do it. Since it's light out, I can get a better look, and that's when I see something scratched down the driver's side.

WHORE.

Well, that's just great. I take pictures of all sides at every angle, then head back inside. After I shower and get dressed, I hear my phone ringing. It's the detective, letting me know he's outside and needs to speak with me.

When I meet him by my car, he informs me of what they'll do with my car, and I relay my conversation with the insurance company. As the tow truck pulls away with my car, he tells me he'll be in touch and we say our goodbyes.

It's now past ten in the morning, and I still haven't heard from Derek. That's not exactly unusual, as they can sleep pretty late on the bus. My boss calls, upset for me, and asks me to keep her informed. Camryn and Mallory have both already called to check on me, and I told them I was fine. I just hope this is as far as this goes.

CHAPTER TWENTY-EIGHT

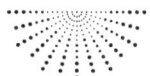

Derek

I wake up in the early afternoon. Time seems to run together when you're on the road. Thank God for Brian keeping us all straight. I take care of some business and throw on some clean clothes, then grab my phone to find I have some missed texts. One is from Kristen, asking me to call her when I get up. I wonder if something else has happened? One is from my mom, and a few are from a number I don't recognize. It looks like they're photos, but I call Chris before dealing with the others.

"Hello?" She sounds drowsy, which is unusual for her in the middle of the day.

"Hey, babe. Did you not sleep good last night? You sound tired."

"Derek? Oh, I'm glad to hear your voice. I was sleeping fine until my car alarm started going off at three this morning. Denny came knocking on my door to tell me it was my car, and you know what? Some asshole threw something through my windshield and slashed my freaking tire! I just don't know what to do, Derek. It scared me so bad. God, I'm glad you asked Denny to keep an eye on me while you were gone. I felt safer having a cop watching out for me, but now...I don't know. I feel like a sitting duck. I'm so ready for you to get home."

I close my eyes and take a deep breath. "I'm sorry, baby. I wish I was there too. Are you going to go stay with Mallory or Camryn? I'd rather you not stay there alone. Did anyone come by besides Denny?"

"Yeah. He called the detective working the case and they impounded my car as evidence. Camryn's coming by later to take me to the rental car place so I have a ride. My insurance company said I can be reimbursed. But Derek, there was a big ass knife in my tire. And when I went out this morning to take pictures for the insurance company, I saw the word 'whore' scratched along my driver's side door. What kind of person does that?"

She's breaking my heart. I feel completely and utterly useless right now. I can't even be there for the girl that holds my heart. I lean my head back on the couch. I'm not even sure what to say.

"A crazy person, baby. Someone not right in the head. I'd really feel better if you don't stay there tonight. You can go stay at my place if you want to. I can call Mom and have her unlock it for you and give you a spare key. Or you can stay in the house with my parents, in my old room. As a matter of fact, if you're not sleeping in my bed, I can just picture you in the bed where I slept in school. Brings back all my high school fantasies." I tease her, trying to lighten the mood. I guess it works because I hear her give a watery laugh.

"You didn't even know me in high school to fantasize about me, you butt. I'm not going to stay at your place without you. I'll stay with one of the girls in the meantime. It's only a few more days, right? I can handle a few more days, but you better let Brian know that I want you all to myself when you get back. All weekend. I already took off work."

"That sounds like a great plan. Three uninterrupted days with you sounds like heaven right now. But the offer still stands if you want to stay at my place." We talk for a few more minutes, then she tells me Camryn's there to take her to pick up her rental. I tell her I love her, and catch movement out of the corner of my eye. I look over and Brian is standing there, drinking a cup of coffee. I put the phone down.

"You wanna tell me what's going on?"

"Everyone else still asleep?" He nods. "Kristen has a stalker. It started a couple months ago. Before I left, a guy she went on a date with got in her apartment and was waiting naked for her on her bed while she was in the shower."

Brian interrupts and asks, "How do you know she didn't invite him?"

I give him a look. "Because Kris and I are together." At this, he spits out his coffee.

"Say again?"

"We're together. Have been for a while now. We've just kept it quiet for Brett's sake. I love her and she loves me, and what's happening to her is driving me crazy. I'm not there for her, and it's like a knife to the heart."

"So, what's going on now?" I tell him about her nearly being robbed the night before, and her car getting trashed this morning. I also tell him about how and when it all started, and the night the kitten was mutilated and left on her front step.

"Is that the night we were supposed to debut Somewhere?" I nod my head. "No wonder your head wasn't in the game that night. Look, I heard you tell her to stay at your place. If she's smart, she'll listen. We only have a week left before we're home for a while. She's gonna be fine in the meantime, but did you have to pick Brett's girl?"

"She's not Brett's girl. She hasn't been for a long time. It's not like I moved in right after they broke up. You make it sound like I swooped right in and took her from him. Brett fucked up and lost her, end of story. I had absolutely nothing to do with their break up; that's all on them. Kris and I sure as hell never planned on being together, it just happened. But I don't regret any of it. She's a great person. Warm, funny, caring, smart, and beautiful. She fills a place in my heart that I didn't know was empty."

"But what about Brett?"

I run my hands over my face. "Brett's been my best friend for longer than I can remember. He's my brother in every way but blood. It's not my intention to hurt him, nor is it hers. We decided to keep this quiet and figure out a good time to let Brett know about us. He was definitely not in a good place when we got together, but he's doing a whole lot better now. I want to make sure it stays that way. Kris and I are fine with only a couple of people knowing. I think after a while, Brett will be okay with it too. At least, I pray that he is. I can't give her up. It would be like ripping my heart out of my chest."

"Is she worth losing your friendship with Brett? Because it may come down to that, you know. Just make sure you know what you gain and what you could lose. Matters of the heart are tricky. You may not be able to have your cake and eat it too." He claps a hand on my shoulder and walks out of the sitting area.

Walking to the back, I see that everyone is still asleep, so I head back to the sitting area and grab a Dr. Pepper out of the fridge. Sitting down, I text my mom, letting her know that I'm okay and that I'm missing her and her fried chicken. That gets a quick laugh sent back from her. Opening up the texts from the unknown number, I scroll down to find a picture of Kris. Actually, there are numerous pictures of Kris. With each picture, I can feel my blood pressure rising. There are pictures of her in her car, outside her apartment, at work, in her apartment. Some are fully clothed and some are of her in her underwear. There are a couple of her hugging a guy, who I recognize as Denny, and one with him kissing the top of her head. What the hell is going on? The next one is a video. I'm not sure I even want to watch, but I hit it anyway. My head explodes. All I can see is the back of a woman with long blonde hair, riding a guy in a bed. I feel like someone's stabbed a knife in my heart. She wouldn't do that to me, I know she wouldn't. For some sick reason, I turn the volume up.

"That's it, Kristen. Ride me, Kristen. Come on my cock, Kristen..." Tears roll down my face, but then it hits me—it's not her. Someone's gone to a lot of trouble to convince me that it's Kristen. I stop the video and read the last message.

SHE IS MINE!

I don't know how long I sit there staring at the phone. I'm trying to wrap my head around all this. This psycho is out of his mind. I'm so in my own head, I don't even notice Jason coming in and sitting in the chair across from me. He snaps his fingers in front of me to get my attention.

"What the hell's up with you? You were staring out into space."

"Dude, some fucked up shit is going on." I tell him what's been going on lately with Kris and her stalker.

"He trashed her car? Damn, she loves that thing."

"Yeah, she does, but it can be repaired. What gets me is what I got today." I hand him my phone after I scroll past the pictures of Kristen. "Someone sent me a bunch of different pictures of Kris. We already know that he hired the PI to follow her, so I assume some of them are from him. There are two of her hugging the neighbor. That cop, Denny, that I asked to keep an eye on her. I think one was from this morning after her car was trashed. He looks like he's wearing pajama pants, and Kris is wearing one of the shirts I left at her place. Then there's this." I hit play on the video, and I watch as his eyes go wide.

"Derek—"

"It's not her, Jason. As much time as I've spent with that girl naked, I know her body pretty well. That chick isn't toned like Kristen is. Also, listen to the guy. He makes sure to say her name. Really? How many times in the middle of sex do you repeat the girl's name and no other endearments? And lastly, she never says a word. Not a sound. Nothing. Kristen's not quiet during sex. Sorry, not buying. That's not my girl fucking this guy. What scares me is the lengths this guy is going to." I scroll to the last of the messages. "This fucking terrifies me. What's going to make this guy stop?"

"Do you still have the PI on retainer?" I nod my head. "Send all this shit to him, maybe he can do something with it. Have you thought about hiring her a bodyguard? I bet our security guys would know someone. It would at least give you peace of mind until we get back home."

"Yeah, it would. Maybe I can talk her into it. She's going to stay with the girls for a few nights."

"Mallory would be the best choice." I give him a look, and he shrugs his shoulders. "She lives in a gated community. She has a state-of-the-art alarm system, and she has a gun and knows how to use it."

I can just imagine the look on my face. "Mallory? Little Mallory is armed?" He nods his head. "Do I even want to know?"

"She had something happen, but it's not my story to tell. I thought she might feel better if she was able to defend herself. I took her to purchase a gun and I taught her how to shoot. Girl's a damn good shot. She's licensed and everything."

"Just how close have you and Mallory gotten, Jason? That's a lot of time to be spending together." I swear he blushes and rubs a hand over the back of his neck. "So, it's like that, huh?"

"Yeah, I think so. Or, at least, I want it to be. We still have to work some stuff out. A lot of it has to do with her past, but I think she may come around, eventually. Otherwise, I'm gonna have blue balls from hell." I laugh at the frustrated look on his face. I pick up my Dr. Pepper can and hold it out. He raises his and I toast us. "To loving good women. May it not bite us in the ass." He chuckles and we bump our cans together.

"Amen to that, brother."

CHAPTER TWENTY-NINE

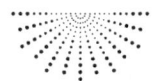

Kristen

I've stayed the last few nights at Mallory's place. Denny's been keeping an eye on my apartment, but so far, nothing else has happened. I just got my car back this morning from the auto shop that Denny had recommended. There's no trace of damage to my baby now. It took a few days before Denny was able to get the surveillance videos from management. He said it was really hard to see anything, but they did see a hooded figure walking around the area. Funny thing was, it looked too small to be Josh. More like a teenager, or a woman, which is just crazy. Does that mean it has nothing to do with my stalker? Have I pissed off someone and not know it? Or was it just random?

I just finished getting off work and I'm heading out to my car. The management got all the lights in the parking lot fixed and my boss makes sure we all leave with someone so we aren't alone. It really freaked her out when she heard what happened.

I say goodbye to the other girls and get in my car to head home. I decide to head to the store right quick because I'm out of creamer for my coffee. I mean, coffee without creamer is a sin. I know that I'm not supposed to go anywhere by myself, but it's pretty early, and there are a ton of people out. So I won't really be alone, right?

I quickly pull into the Walmart that's on my way home and manage to grab a close parking spot. Woohoo! I jump out and round the back, and nearly get clipped by a little black car driving way too damn fast.

"Watch it, asshole!"

I hit the button to lock the car and hitch my purse strap higher on my shoulder. I head in and grab one of the little baskets. Rarely do I ever get out of here with just what I came in for. When I get to the back, I could swear someone's watching me. I try to discreetly look around and see who it is. I probably look like a damn owl, swiveling my head around, but I don't see Josh. I only see long blonde hair on a girl that's standing by the drink display, looking around the display, then she quickly steps back. Okay, that's a little weird. I grab my creamer and put it in the basket and head toward the front of the store. Of course, the aisle I chose goes right by the women's section and I see a cute little pajama set. I reroute and head into the section to check it out. Looking through the racks, I see a flash of blonde hair. Is it weird chick again? I get a better glimpse of her face and she seems familiar to me, but I can't place from where, so I go back to looking through the clothes. Finding a couple sets I like, I throw them in and make a beeline for the checkout. No more distractions. I'm able to get out pretty quickly through the self-checkout line. Digging my keys out of my pocket, I'm almost to my car when I feel someone bump me in the back, hard. So hard, it makes me stumble, and I feel a pain in my side. I glance up and see the blonde again. What the hell? I get in my car and lock the doors, start it up and begin to back out. I'm so distracted that I nearly back into a car going up the aisle. Luckily, the backup camera on the car warns me before I hit them.

I have to get myself together. I check my mirror, then continue to back out of my spot. I try to look around, but the blonde is gone. Poof. My side is burning and I don't know why. As I drive, getting closer to home, the weirder I feel. I pull into my parking spot and move to get out, when I see Denny walking out of his apartment in his uniform. He waves at me before heading to his patrol car. I wave back as I step out, and I stumble. I grab the car door before I hit the ground. I'm light-headed. What the hell is wrong with me? Low blood sugar? Low blood pressure? Dehydration? Blood loss? When that one hits me, I reach down to where my side has been stinging and it comes away red. Oh shit! I try to yell for Denny before he gets in his car, but I don't think I yell out loud enough. If I'm lucky, I can get his attention when he drives by. But he doesn't even look my way. I'm getting even weaker, and end up falling on the pavement. I hear a car slam on its brakes and footsteps running toward me, but I'm fading fast. I see a dark figure stand over me before I pass out.

I'M STARING up at a white ceiling. I blink my eyes slowly and allow myself to adjust to the bright light. I can hear a rhythmic beeping, and it dawns on me where I am. I used to hear the IV pump alarms in my sleep. But why the hell am I in the hospital? I glance around the room and see Mallory and Camryn sitting on a small couch. I must have made a noise or something that catches Camryn's attention because her head pops up and she looks at me.

"Kristen!" Her outburst makes Mallory glance my way too. They both get up and move toward the bed, one on each side.

"How are you feeling?" I take stock of my body. Nothing seems to be bothering me right now, but my mouth is dry as hell. I try to answer Camryn, but nothing comes out. She grabs a small cup with a straw and holds it to my lips, and I take a small sip to wet my mouth. Even though it's tap water, it tastes wonderful. I take a couple more small sips before she moves it away.

"What happened? Why am I here?"

"What's the last thing you remember?"

"I remember getting off work, stopping to pick up some coffee creamer, then going home."

"Well, at some point, someone decided to slice and dice you. The doctor says you have a five-inch knife laceration. Got quite a few stitches too. We don't know when it happened. Denny called us when he saw you laid out in the parking lot next to your car. You were unconscious, so he called for an ambulance. You'd lost quite a bit of blood and went into shock. They got you stitched up and gave you a unit."

"Jesus. Really?" They both nod their heads. Mallory has tears in her eyes, so I reach over to squeeze her hand. I try to think back to what happened, and then it hits me.

"It was the blonde from the store!"

"What blonde?" they both ask.

"While I was in the store, I kept feeling like someone was watching me, following me. I kept seeing a blonde woman in the dairy section, then over by the pajamas. She bumped into me outside, by my car. She hit me hard enough to make me stumble, and I remember my side hurting. I got in the car to head home, but the closer I got, I started feeling weird and was getting lightheaded. I nearly fell out of the car. I tried to get Denny's attention but I couldn't. That's all I can remember. Can I have another drink of water?" Camryn grabs the glass and holds the straw to my lips. "How long have I been here?"

"Only a few hours. They stitched you up in the ER, then sent you up here for the transfusion and observation. More than likely, you'll get to go home in the morning." We all kind of laugh at that. Home in the morning, like that ever happens. It'll be lunchtime at the earliest.

"Has anyone called Derek?" They shake their heads no. "Good. Let's keep it that way. He'll be home in a few days, and there's no point in telling him right now. Can I stay with one of you when I get out?" They both say yes, of course. I see movement by the door and Denny sticks his head in.

"Okay if I come in? Oh, you're awake. Good. I have questions to ask if you're up for it." I nod and he walks in. I tell him the same story that I told the girls. "But I know that blonde from somewhere. I just can't place her."

"It's okay. It'll probably come to you. We've already requested the surveillance video from outside the parking lot. You need to stay out of parking lots, girl. It's where you seem to find all the trouble. I don't think I've ever had to request so many videos in a short amount of time.

"You haven't mentioned this to Derek, have you?" He shakes his head no. "Please, keep it that way. I'll tell him when he gets home. It's only a few days. No need for him to worry."

"I think you need to let him know, but he won't hear it from me." He gives my hand a quick squeeze, winks at the girls and walks out the door.

"That is one hunky cop. I might need to commit a crime so he can use those cuffs on me," Camryn says, and we laugh.

"Maybe Isaac will have some cuffs for you, huh?" She blushes to the roots of her hair.

"Very funny. Now, how about we leave so you can get some sleep. You can barely keep your eyes open. We'll be back in the morning, and I already let Dr. Daniels know what happened. I ran into her downstairs in the cafeteria, and she said for you to take the rest of the week off."

Camryn's right, I'm fading fast. We say our goodbyes and Mallory gives me my phone before she leaves, with instructions to call her if I need anything. I tell her just something to wear home and my toothbrush. Once they leave, I put the phone down and go to sleep.

I'm being chased. First by Josh, then by the blonde. Then the both of them as they laugh at me. Tormenting me. Darkness. A hooded figure. The flash of a knife.

I wake up in a cold sweat, but I finally know who the blonde is. Stephanie, Derek's cheating ex. I know that Derek had some issues with her after their breakup, with her not wanting to let him go, but he hasn't had any recent problems with her that I know of. So why? Why is she coming after me? She can't know that I'm with Derek. Only a few close friends know about us, and none of them would talk to her. We don't exactly run in the same circles, so how on earth does she know? And why would she come after me like this?

CHAPTER THIRTY

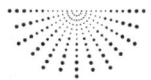

Derek

I've had a bad feeling all night, but I'm not sure why. I didn't get a text from Kristen saying to call her, so I don't think it's her, unless she can't text me. Damn, I'll drive myself crazy if I overthink this. I haven't received any new videos, pictures, or texts of Kristen. I don't know if that's good or bad. I think about checking in with Denny to make sure everything's okay, but it's too late, and it's time for us to go on. We head out onto the stage to rock out with our fans, but I can't shake the feeling.

WE'RE FINALLY DONE for the night, and we rocked the house, just like I knew we would. It's such a rush on nights like these. We're off tomorrow night. We have one more concert, then we'll be home. Thank God. I miss Kristen. I miss hugging her and hearing her laugh. And, of course, I miss fucking her. I'm horny as hell. My right hand and I can only take so much time without her. But mostly, I just want to lay my eyes on her, and not through Skype. Her actually being in front of me before I get inside her.

We head off the stage, back to the green room. I grab my phone out of my pocket and see that I have a text from Kristen. Love you! Talk to you tomorrow. Xoxo. Just reading her text brings a smile to my face, no matter how tired I am.

"Man, you are pussy whipped, dude." Jason chuckles as he walks by me. I look up with the grin on my face and catch Brett looking at me. I'm not even going to worry about that right now. I'm just glad whatever bad feeling I had isn't related to Kristen. We walk into the room and I head to the bar to get a bottle of water, chug it, and get another. It's fucking hot under those lights. My shirt is drenched, and I have a major case of swamp ass. A shower sounds really great right about now.

I look over at the guys and see that Jason and Isaac are talking together in a corner, and Brian is off to the side, looking at his phone. Brett's sitting on a couch surrounded by girls, which isn't surprising. I see movement out of the corner of my eye and more girls are filing in through the door. Seeing the crowd gathered around Brett on the couch, the girls split between me at the bar and Jason and Isaac in the corner. Two blondes are headed right for me, and I brace myself. Some of these girls will take a hint easily, but some are like a dog with a bone. Tenacious does not even begin to describe them, and one of the most persistent ones I have ever met is headed my way. Candy. She's total bombshell material, every inch of her fake, from her overblown lips to her Double D's. I made the mistake in the past of taking her up on what she was offering, and she became a stage-four clinger. She followed us around for months from venue to venue. Each time, she was getting more and more desperate for attention. It got bad enough that Brian had to start banning her from getting backstage. It was such a relief.

For the last six months, I haven't seen hide nor hair of Candy. I thought she had finally gotten over me or found another sucker. I guess I was wrong, because here she comes. I'm not going to lie, the bitch is hot. Tall, slim, huge tits and a nice ass. She's wearing what I guess is a dress. It looks more like a stretched out tube top. If it goes down a centimeter, her tits are going to pop out. I swear, the only thing holding it up are her hard nipples. She looks like a high-dollar hooker.

I see the smile on her face and the look in her eyes, like she has me right where she wants me. I try to catch Brian's attention before this gets too far, but he's talking to some woman that came in. Security is nowhere to be seen. Fuck, this could get ugly, fast. Maybe if I can circumvent her, I can avoid this train wreck. I turn to go the other way, but Jason and Isaac, with their following, have made their way to the bar, cutting off my escape. I turn the other way, but it's too late. Her perfume cloud precedes her arms coming up around my neck. I raise my hands and grab them before she can wrap herself around me like a vine.

"Hello, lover," she purrs, trying to push herself on me. I continue to hold her arms and step back from her to keep my distance. The last time the crazy bitch got her hands on me, there were pictures all over social media about us being a couple. That was a fucking joke, and what got her banned.

"Candy, how the hell did you get back here? You know you've been banned from coming backstage. You need to leave, and do it now."

I happen to catch Brian looking this way, and I can only

pray that he sees the look on my face to know something's wrong. He does. He signals someone and heads toward me at a brisk pace. Thank you, God, for small favors. I see someone from security trailing him.

"Candy, you know you're not supposed to be back here. You need to remove yourself from the premises. This gentleman will make sure you leave. Do not come back, or I will have you arrested. I believe you still have a restraining order?"

The security guard gently touches her arm to move her away, and she starts to fight against him. You can tell he's trying to be gentle since she's a woman, but she's fighting like a hell cat. One guy isn't going to do it. I can see other security guards rush into the room, and it takes three grown men to wrangle her. Before it's over, they have her on the floor. Her dress, well, it went up and down. Her tits are out for everyone to see, and we now know she's not wearing underwear. I already knew she likes a Brazilian. They finally get her up off the floor and out the door with everything showing. It's definitely put a damper on everyone's mood. I head for the door and notice that Brett is no longer sitting on the couch. I nod toward Jason and Isaac to let them know I'm leaving. They return the nod and head my way. I guess we're all tired tonight.

We don't have to head out until tomorrow, so Brian secured us hotel rooms for the night. We're supposed to have a car waiting to take us to the hotel since the tour bus would stick out like a sore thumb. Jason, Isaac, and I head outside and see that there is only one car waiting. The driver gets out and approaches us.

"I thought there were two cars? Gonna be kind of cramped for six of us to ride in there."

"There were two cars, sir. One gentleman took the other car

with his lady friends. They've already left for the hotel." Huh, so that's where Brett had disappeared to. Off with the groupies. I pull out my phone and text Brian, letting him know that if he's riding with us, he needs to get his ass out here. He finally makes it outside, and we load up to head to the hotel. It'll be nice to sleep in a real bed before we go out for our last spot on this tour. We're so close to the end, I can almost taste it.

When we arrive, a staff member is waiting for us with keys to our rooms. I don't know how Brian handles all this, but I thank God that he does. I'm dying for a shower and a soft mattress. I'm glad we don't have to share rooms like we did when we first started out. Talk about not being able to sleep with all of us snoring.

I go into my room and avoid tripping on my bag that's been placed in the middle of the floor. I go straight for the shower. As soon as steam is pouring out of the stall, I remove my clothes and get in. The hot water beating down on my tired body feels so good. When I'm finally clean, I just stand under the spray, letting the hot water run over me, relaxing me. Until I think of Kris. I palm my cock and slowly start to stroke it from root to tip. I imagine Kris down on her knees, with her big blue eyes looking up at me. Her hand wraps around the base while she runs her pink tongue around the head, then she takes me into her hot little mouth. Slowly moving back and forth, she takes me inch by inch until her mouth reaches her hand. The next stroke of her mouth brings her nose to the hairs at the root. I can feel her throat swallow around my cock as she cups my balls. Placing my hands in her hair, I begin to thrust my hips. With her every little moan, I thrust a little deeper, a little harder. She takes her free hand and places it between her legs. When she closes her eyes, I can tell she's close, and so am I. I thrust one last time and feel my cum shoot down her throat in hard spurts.

I slowly come back to myself, breathing hard. Fuck, I miss her. I clean up the mess I made and grab the towel to dry off. Grabbing my phone and charger, I set them next to the bed. When I climb under the covers, I hear the noises from next door. Girly giggles and moans. Guess that means Brett's room is next to mine, and our beds are against the same wall. That's just great.

I turn on the TV so I can drown out the noise. Finding an episode of Ink Master, I leave it there. Maybe I'll get a new tattoo when I get back to Dallas, something that reminds me of Kris. Maybe her name. I pick up my phone and go to the message she had left me earlier. I text her back. Love you too. Miss you so much. I'm counting down the hours until I can hold you in my arms. Kiss you. Do dirty, dirty things to your body. I add an eggplant and peach emoji and hit send. I turn off the light and settle in. It doesn't take long before I'm out.

CHAPTER THIRTY-ONE

Kristen

I actually slept pretty good, considering I was in the hospital. Every two hours, the nurse would pop her head in. Every four hours was vital signs. Some I don't remember, due to the pain medication they gave me during the night. I stretch a little and gasp at the stabbing pain in my right side. The pain meds have definitely worn off. The nurse comes in with my next dose of IV antibiotics. I hope it's the last dose, because then they can take my IV out. She checks my incision and changes the dressing. This is the first time I've gotten to see where I was cut with the knife. Whoever stitched me up did a really good job. The scar shouldn't be too bad. I don't notice any signs of infection, which is good. It means I can get out of here faster. She's fast and efficient, which I appreciate.

"Can I get you anything else before I leave?"

"On your way back down here, could you get me something

for pain?" Hopefully, they have oral pain medication ordered for me. She nods and leaves, but then Camryn enters.

"A venti caramel macchiato and an omelet from the grill downstairs. Made with fresh cracked eggs, no powder in sight." She grins at me.

"God bless you." I take a sip of the coffee and moan. A little taste of heaven. I open up the container and get a whiff of the goodness inside. An omelet with bell pepper, onion, sausage, and tons of cheesy goodness. Nothing could possibly taste better. "Thank you so much."

"Well, I couldn't in good conscience let you starve. Mallory will be here shortly. She was gonna stop by your apartment and grab you some clothes and stuff." I nod my head and continue to stuff my face. Camryn turns on the TV and finds a talk show to watch while I eat. Finally, Mallory shows up with my clothes.

We call the nurse down to unhook my IV so I can get in the shower. Luckily, she applied a waterproof bandage on top of my sutures so I don't have to worry about getting it wet. I can't have my IV taken out just yet, as the doctor had ordered a specific number of antibiotics that I had to have prior to discharge. The girls help me as much as they can to get me cleaned up. It feels freaking great to be clean. Mallory was nice enough to grab my shampoo, conditioner, and body wash, so I don't have to use the generic stuff the hospital supplies. Camryn helps me wash my hair, as it hurts when I raise my right arm up. Luckily, Mallory brought me a pair of black yoga pants instead of jeans so the band wouldn't rub on my wound.

There's nothing to do in a hospital but wait. My next antibiotic isn't due for three more hours, and the doctor still has to check me over before I can be discharged. I send Camryn and Mallory home, telling them I'll call them when it's time to go. No point in all of us being bored to death. I fall asleep watching crappy daytime television, and wake up when the nurse comes in to administer my last dose of antibiotics. Finally, around three, the doctor comes in. Giving my wound a quick look, he tells me I'm okay to leave. Five minutes is all it takes for him to figure that out and he's out the door. I grab my phone and text the girls to let them know that I'm free to leave. I still have to wait for my discharge paperwork, and depending on how busy my nurse is, it could take a while. Mallory and Camryn arrive about a half an hour later and the nurse has my discharge papers a few minutes later.

We hit the pharmacy to pick up my pain medication and antibiotics before we head back to my apartment. Apparently, the girls were busy while I was gone. My island is covered with junk food. I guess we're going to pig out this afternoon. We find a movie on Netflix to watch, and Camryn orders us some pizza and wings. We're about halfway into The Hangover when the pizza arrives. My mouth starts watering when the smell of garlic, cheese, and pepperoni hits me. I'm going to put on ten pounds before the night is over.

"Y'all know you don't have to stay the whole night, right?"

"Of course we do."

"What are friends for? Please. And you have all the good food here. You're not getting rid of us that easily."

"I couldn't ask for better friends. I love y'all." I can tell my speech is getting a little slurred. I don't handle pain medication very well. I figure I'll be sound asleep in the next ten to fifteen minutes, so I grab my phone off the table and scroll through it. Shit. I missed a text from Derek. Love you too. Miss you so much. I'm counting down the hours until I can hold you in my arms. Kiss you. Do dirty, dirty things to your body. The eggplant and peach make me giggle. Mallory looks back at me.

"Sorry. Derek sent me something sunny. I mean, funny." She gives me a quick smile and turns back around. I make a decision and I head into my bedroom and grab the selfie stick out of the drawer. I take off my top and my bra. Not easy with the stitches, but the pain meds are kicking in and I don't feel anything but a slight twinge in my side. I take off my yoga pants and lay in the bed, leaving me in only my lacy blue panties. I put my phone on the selfie stick and try to do a seductive pose. After about five different pictures, I give up. Hopefully, one is good enough. I grab my phone and lay the stick down. The first two pictures are the exact opposite of sexy, but the third looks hot, I think. I tweak the filters on my phone and send it to Derek. I can't wait Xoxo. I get up and go to the bathroom, get redressed, and head back out to the living room.

"You okay?"

"I'm good." Whoa. Yes, I'm a little bit high from the meds. I lay back on the couch to watch the movie. Before I realize it, I'm asleep.

MALLORY SHAKES ME, and I come awake with a start. "The electricity went out, but it's only in this building. I can see the lights on in the other complexes. That means your alarm doesn't work. I think we need to leave and head to my place."

"Okay. Let me grab some stuff for tomorrow." I use the flashlight on my phone to move around and grab some clothes out of my drawers. I'm throwing them in the bag that I brought home from the hospital when I hear glass break. "Camryn? Mallory?" I don't get an answer. I grab the bag and head to the living room. Mallory's waiting right next to the door and touches my arm, making me jump. She places a hand over my mouth.

"Shhh. There's someone out back. We need to go out the front. Be quiet." She grabs my hand and we head for the front door, where Camryn's standing. Camryn quietly turns the lock and the click sounds unusually loud. She opens the door, and I'm glad it doesn't squeak. We go out as quietly as possible, and Mallory shuts the door behind us. Jogging to Mallory's car, Camryn gets in the back seat and I get in the front. Camryn pulls her phone out and calls 911, while I text Denny. I see that his patrol car is gone, so I know he's working. I let him know that we are heading to Mallory's apartment, if he or the other officers need me. I don't see any movement as I stare out into the darkness.

Mallory starts the car and we head out of the lot to the road. Her apartment is only a few minutes down the road, but it's kind of in the middle of nothing. It's a pretty new development, and the only things around are two other complexes that are being built. I can see the street lights in the distance, leading to her apartment. My phone rings, and it's Derek.

"Hey, babe."

"Hey, Kris. Um, things kinda came to a head today. Brett…" He trails off, and when I look up, I notice a truck in the side mirror, barreling toward us with no lights on. The moon hits it just right for me to see it.

"What the fuck? Mallory, there's a truck headed right for us." As soon as I finish the sentence, the truck is beside us and clips our fender. We scream out, but Mallory manages to keep the car on the road and straightens us out. I can feel the car accelerate, but it's no match for the truck. The truck swerves at us again and hits us just right. The car spins around, and the back tires slide off the embankment on the side of the road. We're rolling. I feel something hit me in the head, and the crunch of metal. Screaming. Then everything goes black.

Camryn

I hit my head, then feel something wet running down my face. Mallory and Kris are out cold. I can hear someone yelling, and it dawns on me that it's Derek on Kristen's phone.

"Derek! Oh God." I try to find my phone, but we're upside down, and it's dark. "I can't find my phone. I need to call for help." I remember that in Mallory's car, you can push for 911, but I can't reach it from where I am. I reach to undo my seatbelt and I fall to the roof. Fuck, that hurt. I crawl toward the front of the car and try to squeeze between the top of the seats and the roof where it's crushed in. I can see the button lit up on the rearview mirror. I reach my hand out, but I'm still too far away. I try to squeeze between the seats again, but there's not enough room. I see a hand come up beside mine and reach the button. I look and see Mallory looking at me.

"Thank God, Mal. Are you okay?"

"I think so. What about Kris?"

"I don't know." I can still hear Derek in the background, then Mallory is talking with the 911 operator. I glance out through what is left of the window on my right and see legs walking toward us.

"Mallory! Someone's coming!" Oh God. Is it the person who ran us off the road? Mallory begins to move around, and somehow gets the console between the two front seats open. I hear a thunk, then a chambering of a bullet. The person is getting closer. He stops on my side of the car, by the passenger door, squats down and looks in. Motherfucker! It's Josh. That fucking psycho. He sees me looking at him, and he grins. Man, this dude is fucking crazy. He stands back up and tries to open Kristen's door, but it's jammed. I hear him stomping and cursing, then the breaking of more glass. I watch as his hands go through the window and starts pulling on Kristen.

"Stop it, you asshole! You're gonna hurt her!" He doesn't listen, just keeps pulling. The only thing keeping her in the car is her seat belt. He finally realizes this and pulls out a knife. Out of the corner of my eye, I can see Mallory squirming around in her seat. There's no way she can shoot him without hitting Kris. I crawl toward the window that's broken, which is on the opposite side of Kristen and Josh. I feel something slice through my cheek and hiss at the pain, but it doesn't stop me. By the time I get out, Josh has Kristen halfway out of the car.

"Leave her alone!" But he doesn't even flinch when I yell. He just keeps pulling. I feel a hand grab my leg and I jump and fall on my ass. Mallory is halfway out of her broken window with a gun in her right hand and using her left to try and pull herself through. I reach down to help her, and she yelps when I grab her hand. But there's no time to waste. Mallory clears the car and stands up with the gun ready and aimed.

"Hey, you fucker! Drop my friend." The gun goes off. I can hear the sirens in the distance. I try to stand, but I can't put any weight on my leg.

"Stay there, Camryn. I'm going on the other side to check on Kris. Looks like the Calvary is on its way." I can see the lights from the cop cars. Mallory moves around to the other side. "She's breathing, but she's bleeding pretty badly. I can't tell from where. It's pooling underneath her. I can't move her by myself. I think my wrist is broken."

I pull myself up and try to stand. "And Josh?"

"I don't care about that fucker, but I don't think he'll make it with that hole in his head." The cops are running toward us now. Mallory puts her gun on what's left of the car, and I breathe out a sigh of relief.

CHAPTER THIRTY-TWO

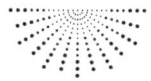

Derek

We're on the bus, headed to our last stop in Tulsa for our last gig this tour. It won't be over soon enough. My last night away from her. But I still haven't shaken the bad feeling I had last night, and Brett's acting like a bug crawled up his ass. Every time I look at him, he's giving me the stink-eye. We finally pull up outside the venue and get off the bus. The roadies have been unloading the stuff to get us set up, and we head in so we can do a sound check.

I check my phone, but Kris hasn't texted me back from last night. The equipment is ready and I pull out my guitar. I run through a few chords, and so does Isaac. Jason gets behind the drums and warms up. We're just waiting for Brett to get on stage so we can get this done. I realize that my phone is in my pocket, so I take it out and lay it on the amp next to me. I'm moving my guitars around when Brett finally graces us with his presence. About the time he walks by me, my phone dings with a message and my heart stops. I stare at him and he stares right back. Then he glances down at my phone, grabs it up and swipes his thumb across the screen. I begin to walk toward him when he looks at me with hate in his eyes. I stop in my tracks. I can only assume that Kristen texted me back.

"You cocksucking motherfucker!" He throws my phone at me and I see the text that Kristen sent me. Son of a bitch. Not that I don't appreciate a naked pic of my girl, it's just that the timing really sucks. I put the phone in my pocket and look at Brett.

"Brett—" I start to say, but he cuts me off.

"How long have you been fucking my girl, Derek? How long have you been betraying me? Have you been fucking her all along?" He's seething, and his chest is pumping up and down with his heavy breathing.

"She's not your girl anymore, Brett. That's on you. We didn't get together until a few months ago, and don't you fucking dare insinuate that she has been doing anything wrong. You were the cheater in y'all's relationship. You fucked up the best thing that has ever happened to you." He lets out a primal scream and charges me. I try to block him as much as I can, but he lands a shot to my jaw that rattles me. I step back and hit him with a left hook. We continue to exchange blows until Jason and Isaac pull us apart. Jason is holding Brett back.

"I fucking trusted you, and you took her away from me. Why? Why would you do that? You're my friend! My brother!"

I shake Isaac off. "I didn't take her from you, Brett. You lost her all on your own. We never meant to hurt you, but we love each other."

Jason lets him go. "Fuck you, Derek." He walks off the stage. I hang my head and run my hand across my face. Fuck. This is not how I wanted him to find out. Jason and Isaac are just standing there, not knowing what to do or say. I move my hand to my jaw and try to work out some of the soreness.

"You're gonna have a black eye, man. We need to get you some ice, and we need to track down Brett."

"Why do we need to track down Brett? Why are y'all not doing your sound check?" Brian asks as he heads on stage. "What the fuck happened to you, Derek?"

"Brett happened."

"Fuck. What set him off?" He looks at me. "Found out, huh? Told you this might blow up in your face. I'll get security looking for him. We have two hours before those doors open." He turns around and walks off stage.

"Wait, let me get this straight. You and Kristen are together? Since when? And how the hell did you keep this from us?" Isaac looks at me, then Jason. Jason is looking away from Isaac and rubbing a hand on the back of his neck. "Fuck, Jason. You knew? Brian obviously knows. I guess it was just me and Brett outta the loop. I can understand why you left him out, but why me?"

"We hadn't planned on anyone knowing for a while. We wanted Brett in a better place before we told him. We were worried that it might send him off the deep end. Jason found out by accident."

"Jesus, what a clusterfuck of epic proportions. We need to find him and get this concert over with. Then we can get all this straightened out."

We finished as much of the sound check as we could without Brett, but with fifteen minutes until showtime, Brett is still nowhere to be found. Brian comes and tells us that he's canceling the show, and we'll have to reschedule for another night. I hate to disappoint our fans, but we can't play without our lead singer. We start to head back to the green room as we wait for Brian. I decide to call Kris, to warn her that the cat is out of the bag, so I grab my phone out of my pocket and scroll through my contacts. I touch the button to call her.

"Hey, babe."

"Hey, Kris. Um, things kinda came to a head today. Brett saw the picture you sent me and he went off the deep end." I can hear her saying something about a truck. "Kris? Babe?" The next thing I hear is metal on metal and someone scream. "Kris!" I hear the metal scraping and glass breaking. Girls screaming. All I can do is scream her name into the phone as I sink to my knees. Jason and Isaac have rushed over, and each have a hand on my shoulder. Finally, there's silence. "Kris, baby, answer me, please. I need to know you're okay. Please, baby." Tears are streaming down my face. "Baby, please, I need you. Don't leave me, baby. It'll kill me."

Jason takes the phone away from me and continues to listen. I'm beyond being able to. I can't lose her. She's my everything. Please, God, don't take her away from me. I can't remember the last time I prayed, but I'm on my knees praying now.

"I can hear Camryn talking...and there's Mallory. I still haven't heard Kris, though. Camryn said there's someone walking toward them. Motherfucker, it's that fucker Josh! He hit them. I don't know what he's doing, but Camryn's cussing him out." He puts it on speaker so we can all hear. All I can see is red. He's trying to get my girl. I can hear Camryn yelling at him, her voice breaking as she can't do anything.

I feel so helpless. There's nothing I can do for her. I'm failing her. Then I hear the shot and my heart stops. I can't breathe. All

I can hear is the pounding of my heart and can see nothing but Kristen's face.

One of the guys slap me on the back and I take a breath. I look up into Jason's face. "I think Mallory shot him, but I'm not sure. I can't make out what's happening, but I can hear the girls' voices." I finally tune back into what's happening. The sirens are getting louder and louder until it's all we can hear. Jason hangs up the phone and throws it back to me. "Call your cop friend. I'm gonna find Brian and tell him we need to get the hell home right now." He hurries out of the room.

I don't know what's happening. I'm walking around in a fog. All I can think about is Kristen. I'm staring at the pictures I have of her in my phone when Denny calls to tell me that the girls are alive and being taken to the hospital. Mallory and Camryn have non-life-threatening injuries, but Kristen was seriously injured.

Somehow, Brian got us a car and we're heading from Tulsa to Dallas. Now we're hauling ass down I-75 toward home.

Jason and Isaac have come with me. Brian stayed behind because Brett was still MIA, not answering his phone or returning messages. But I don't care about that. All I can think is that the love of my life may be dying and I'm not there. I'm not holding her hand, telling her I love her. Telling her everything will be okay. At this point, I can only hope and pray.

Denny is keeping us as up-to-date as he can. He's at the hospital with the girls. Kristen is currently in surgery. Apparently, when she was pulled out of the car, a piece of metal lacerated her liver, reopened her previous wound (what previous wound?), and she has some bleeding on the brain. The more he tells me, the more I cry. He doesn't have any more details than that. It's just a waiting game now for the surgeon to come out.

Jason asks about Mallory. "Mallory has a slight concussion and a broken wrist. Camryn has a broken ankle and a laceration to her face. They're both gonna be fine. I'm trying to keep the questioning to a minimum until Kris gets out of surgery. I'll call you with any updates that I get."

The drive home is the longest of my life. I check my phone every few minutes, but there are no calls, no texts, no updates. Finally, we roll up into the drive for the hospital. Before the car has even come to a complete stop, I'm out the door. The automatic doors can't open quick enough and I clip my shoulder on it on the way through. This late at night, there's no one manning the front desk, so I grab my phone and call Denny.

"What floor?"

"Surgery is on second. Mallory and Camryn are on the fifth." I run down the hall to the elevator, earning me a dirty look from a lady with a trash cart. I can hear footsteps pounding behind me. I slide to a stop in front of the elevator and push the button, just as Jason and Isaac come to a stop behind me. It takes forever for the doors to open. If I knew where the stairs were, I would have gone there instead. Finally, they open.

"Kris is still in surgery on two. The girls are on five." I push the two and one of the others push five. We reach the second floor and I hurry off down the hall, trying to find the waiting room. I can hear someone behind me. I figure it's going to be Isaac, with Jason going up to see the girls. I find the waiting room and Denny is sitting there. He stands up when we come in and walks over to me and pulls me into a hug.

"Any word?"

"Someone came out a little while ago to say they were getting close to finishing. She's hanging in there." My knees go weak with relief and I collapse in the nearest chair. Now, we wait.

After an eternity, the doors finally open and a man in scrubs walks through. "Family of Kristen Davidson?" We nod our heads. "I'm Dr. Blankenship. I'm one of the surgeons who operated on Miss Davidson. She made it through. It was touch and go for a while; she lost a lot of blood. From what we were able to see, she was cut by a piece of metal from the car. It was very deep. It reopened her previous injury and nicked her liver. We got the bleeding from her liver stopped, and she also had a very large hematoma that was pushing on her brain. More than likely a result of the impact during the accident. We had to drill a small hole in her skull to drain the blood and relieve the pressure. We're going to place her in ICU and keep her in a medically-induced coma to allow her brain to heal. We'll keep her medicated and pain-free, and will be monitoring her for any signs of bleeding or infection. She will be kept comfortable. After forty-eight hours, we plan to take her off the medications that are keeping her asleep and allow her to wake up naturally. But I want to warn you, she'll be on a ventilator. There will be lots of tubes and machines that she will be hooked up to. After we take her off the medications, she may not wake up right away. The brain acts differently with each person. When she wakes up, we'll know the extent of the damage to her brain." He shakes our hands and tells us that she'll be in recovery for an hour, then transferred to ICU on the third floor.

Instead of heading to the third floor right away, we head up to the fifth to check on Camryn and Mallory. I text Jason, and he lets me know that Camryn is in 504 and Mallory is in 506. The elevator arrives quickly and we head up to five, going to

Mallory's room first. Jason is sitting in the chair beside her bed. She's sleeping, with her splinted left arm elevated on a pillow.

"I'm heading to Camryn's room," Isaac says as he backs out the door.

"Okay, Denny, what the fuck is going on?" He takes a deep breath.

"From what I can tell, somehow the power got knocked out at Kristen's apartment. Someone broke the back slider onto her patio and the girls went out the front. One of them called 911 and Kristen called me. I was out on patrol, but I was close. They decided to head to Mallory's apartment when they were struck by a truck, which was found at the scene. From initial reports, the truck struck their car, causing it to go off the embankment. It flipped several times. Mallory was driving, Kris was in the passenger seat, and Camryn was in the back. Now, until we talk to the girls, we don't know exactly what happened after that. When the responding officer arrived, Camryn was on one side of the car and Mallory was on the other with a body lying on the ground. Kristen was lying halfway out of the car. There was a gun lying on the ground, and the man from the truck was deceased. He was identified as Josh Anderson. He was DOA. One bullet through the head."

"Jesus fucking Christ. What were they talking about, a previous wound that Kristen had?"

"Fuck. She was gonna tell you when you got back. She got knifed in the parking lot the night before and had to get stitches. They kept her overnight for observation. She went home yesterday." He glances at his watch.

"I shot him in the head because that was the only shot I could get. The rest of him was hidden behind the car. I just knew I couldn't let him take Kris." All of us turn to look at

Mallory. Jason moves to her side and picks up her hand. She looks at him, then at us. "Is she okay? What about Camryn?"

"She's fine. I checked on her a few minutes ago and she was sleeping. Isaac is in there with her now."

"Kris had to get her liver fixed, and something about relieving pressure in her brain. I'm going to head down to ICU. The doctor said she would be in recovery for about an hour before they moved her. It should be about that time. I want to be there when they roll her in." I go and give Mallory a quick kiss on the forehead. "Thank you for saving her." I turn and head out of the room.

I make it to ICU, and they direct me to the room she'll be in. It's a nice big room, with a little couch that spreads out into a little bed. I sit down and one of the nurses brings me a pillow and blanket. I give her a smile and a thank her as she quietly walks out. Eventually, I can hear the squeaking of shoes on the linoleum and the door opens so they can wheel the bed with Kristen inside. Four others come in with her and I can't get a good look at her with them hovering around. I finally give up and sit down so they can finish what they need to.

Finally, the room quiets and I look up. Only one nurse is left in the room, and she's on her computer. I stand up and move toward her bed, and my breath catches in my throat. She's so still, but I can see the even rise and fall of her chest. Her head is wrapped with some white dressing and her eyes are black. She has a tube coming out of her mouth that is attached to one of the machines. The blanket is drawn up to her chest so I can't see the rest of her. Her arms are lying on top of the blankets, tubes running in both arms; one clear, one red.

The nurse begins to explain to me what is happening. The tube is helping her breathe. She's receiving the last unit of blood that was ordered. One of the machines she is hooked up to will monitor her blood pressure, respirations, and oxygen levels. She tells me to call her if I need anything and that she will be monitoring from a station down the hall. I thank her and she leaves the room. I grab a chair and pull it up next to her bed. I hold her hand and I pray.

CHAPTER THIRTY-THREE

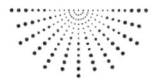

Brett

I storm off the stage with the knife stuck in my back. That motherfucker. How the ever-loving fuck could he do this to me? Betray me this way? All I can see in front of me is red. With every step I take, the knife twists deeper. I see a side door and slam into it, making my way outside and toward the back. I flag down a cab and tell him to take me to the closest bar. We go a couple miles and he lets me out at a pretty popular looking place, judging by the number of people going in. I head in and take a seat at the corner of the bar that's sort of hidden in the shadows. The bartender comes over to me pretty quickly.

"What can I get ya?"

"Patron. Make it a double and keep 'em coming." I get my wallet out and lay a hundred on the bar top. "Keep me in drink and that'll be your tip. And I'm not driving anywhere." She nods her head, turns around and grabs a bottle and glasses. She pours one glass and I slam it as she pours the next. She then hands me another glass and sets it down. "That's just water." She pours me another. I can feel my phone vibrating in my pocket. I know the guys are trying to reach me, but right now, I don't give a flying fuck what they want. Fuck them. Fuck the fans. Fuck Derek. Fuck the world.

I don't know how long I've been sitting here, but I'm drunk as hell. I don't think I can get off this stool and not fall straight to the ground. And I've got to take a piss. I start to slide off the stool and a hand on my shoulder stops me from sliding to the floor. I glance up and see two of Brian. Or is that three?

"Jesus, Brett. What the fuck? How much have you had to drink? And you can't answer your fucking phone?"

"Didn't want to answer it," I slur. He helps me stand up. "I gotta take a piss." Brian leads me toward a hallway and through a door. Luckily, there's no one else in the bathroom with us.

"I'm not holding your dick for you. Don't piss all over yourself. I have to ride in the car with you and I don't wanna smell you." I fumble around with my jeans and get them down. When I finish, I work to adjust my clothing. When I finally manage to zip up my pants, Brian leads me outside, to the car sitting at the curb. He shoves me in the back and says something to the driver. I feel us move and I lay my head against the seat. The more the car moves, the more nauseous I get. We finally stop in front of a hotel. Brian opens the door and gets out, so I scoot along the seat to follow him, but I can't get my legs under me. Brian grabs my arm and hauls me out. He leads me to the elevator and we get on. As we start to move, I try not to puke. We finally get off the roller coaster ride of an elevator and Brian leads me down the hall, opens the door, and shoves me inside. "Sober the fuck up, Brett. We leave for home in the morning." And with that, he slams the door. I can't hold it anymore and head into the bathroom. I barely make it to the toilet before I puke up my toenails.

I don't know how long I've been in here, lying on the cold tile floor, but I know I need to get up. I slowly move to a sitting position and see if it upsets my stomach. So far, so good. I slowly stand up. Good, my body is cooperating. I head over to the shower and get in. I don't even wait for the water to warm up, I just get in under the icy spray. The water starts to warm and I soak it in.

When I finish, I dry off and head out to get some clothes from my bag. I dress and sit on the edge of the bed, just as Brian walks through the door. I can tell he's pissed just by looking at him.

"You let me down tonight, Brett. You let the band down. You let the fans down." I start to argue that Derek let me down when he holds a hand up to stop me from speaking. "I know you're hurting right now. I know you think that Derek betrayed you, but you're a professional. You don't let your personal feelings get in the way of your job. But that's exactly what you did. You stormed off, causing all of us to worry about you. And where do I find you? At a bar, getting trashed. We're flying home in the morning. I had to cancel tonight's performance and we'll have to reschedule. You let a lot of fans down tonight. I told them there was an emergency and some of the band members had to leave. Hopefully, that will be enough to satisfy them."

"Emergency? That's what you want to call this?" I laugh.

"No. You weren't the emergency. Kristen and two of her friends were in a car accident. She's in bad shape and had to be rushed into surgery. Derek left to be with her and the boys went with him. They're in a car headed for Dallas right now. I couldn't go because I had to find your drunk ass and make sure you were okay. We fly out at 8:50 in the morning, but we leave here at six. Make sure you're fucking ready. I ordered you some room service. Eat and drink plenty of water." He turns around and leaves the room.

I'm in shock. Kris is hurt? Fuck. I lose track of time as I sit here thinking. Room service arrives, and I do as Brian said. I eat what I can and drink the two bottles of water they brought up before I crawl into bed. I guess the alcohol is still working on me and I start to feel sleepy. I turn on the TV and drift off to an episode of Street Outlaws.

I WAKE to the room's 5:30 wake up call. I thank the voice on the other end and hang up the phone. I shower and get dressed, and all I can think about is Kristen. I grab my phone and see that I haven't had another call or text since last night. At 5:55, Brian's knocking on my door. I grab my bag and we head out to the car waiting for us downstairs.

"Have you heard anything about Kristen?"

"She made it through surgery. She's in ICU in a medically-induced coma right now." He's being very cold toward me, and I don't blame him.

It's that way until we land in Dallas. Making our way through the terminal to baggage, we grab our things and head out to the car Brian has waiting for us.

"What hospital is she in?"

"Baylor, but we're not headed there. I'm taking you home."

"Brian, I have to go to the hospital. I need to see her."

"I don't think it's a good idea right now, not with what

happened yesterday. No one needs the added stress. Go home and chill. I'll keep you updated."

We pull up in front of my house and I get out and slam the door. I head into my house, but before I shut the door, he pulls away. I'm trying to decide on what to do. My first thought is to get in my truck and haul ass to the hospital. But then, I think about what Brian said and decide to stay home. I try to think of things to do around the house to take my mind off Kris, and I end up in my music room. I pick up my guitar and start strumming as I stare out the window, watching the day go by. I start to form a melody and grab some paper and a pencil to jot down the ideas. I hear my phone ding and see that Brian has texted me. No change. I go back to making music. It's what I'm good at.

I've waited as long as I possibly can. I can't stand it, so I head to the hospital. I walk in to her room and find it empty. My breath lodges in my chest when I see her lying there. God, how could this happen to her? What has she ever done to anyone? She looks so helpless hooked up to all these machines, her head wrapped in a bandage, a tube coming out of her mouth. I walk over to the bed. The blankets are pulled up to her chest, but her arms are lying on top. I run my finger up and down her arm, just to feel her warmth. What I wouldn't give to have her beautiful blue eyes open and see me. See her smile at me.

"Hey, Kris," I whisper. "It's me. I just needed to see you. I'm sorry this happened to you. You are the good in this world. Lord knows, you're the best thing that ever happened to me and I threw it away. What I wouldn't give to take that night back, but what's done is done." I catch my breath and feel the tears sliding down my cheeks. I take the hand that's not touching her and wipe my face. "I want you to be happy, but I want you to be happy with me, as selfish as that is."

I happen to catch something out of the corner of my eye. I jerk my head in that direction and see Derek standing there with his arms crossed over his chest.

CHAPTER THIRTY-FOUR

Derek

It's been nearly two days since my world was turned upside down. I've been living at the hospital. Kris has remained stable. It's just hard to see her lying there, not moving, smiling, or talking. The nurse told me this morning that they would be taking her off the medications that are keeping her asleep. She did make sure to remind me that she may not wake up right away. It could be a couple more days before she completely wakes. I'm just ready for her to open her eyes and look at me.

Brian, Jason, and Isaac have been in and out, keeping me company. Mainly, it's been Brian. Jason's been up in Mallory's room, and Isaac's been with Camryn. Both girls are scheduled to be released today. Neither had to have surgery for their broken bones, just set and casted. Mallory hasn't had any complications from her concussion, but Camryn had to have her faced stitched up. Her cut went from her temple, down her cheek and to her chin. Luckily, they had a surgeon who trained with a plastic surgeon, so hopefully her scar will be minimal. Jason texts me that the girls have been released and I head up there to see them off.

Mallory and Camryn were finally able to give their statement to the detective over the case. It just happened to be the same detective that was overseeing Kristen's stalker. We all have the fear that Mallory may be charged with something, even though she was saving her friend. But a man did die at her hands. The information will be given to the DA's office to see what will happen.

I head back down to Kristen's room. I don't want to take the chance of missing the doctor. I walk to her door and stop short. Brett's standing next to her bed with his back to the door. I can hear him talking softly to her, but I can't make out what he's saying. He reaches out and runs his finger up and down her arm. It pisses me off that he's touching her. I just want to rip him away and throw him out of the room, but I keep myself in check. He finally looks in my direction.

"You look like shit." He turns back around to look at Kris.

"Wow, a compliment right out of the gate." I rub a hand through my hair. "I haven't left since I got here. That couch bed isn't long enough, or comfortable." There's an uncomfortable silence in between us. He's the last person I expected to see here after the way we left things. But, then again, this is Kristen we're here for, and he still loves her.

"What are you doing here, Brett?"

"I needed to see her. I can't believe this happened to her. She doesn't deserve this."

"No, she doesn't, but at least the fucker that did it is dead." He gives me a questioning look. "Mallory shot him."

"Wait. What the fuck are you talking about? What do you mean, Mallory shot someone?"

I head over to the sofa thing and sit down. "What do you know?"

"The girls were in a car accident. Kris was seriously injured, and the other girls had minor injuries."

"I guess I'll have to start a little further back. Kristen had a stalker." I fill him in on everything that has happened, from the beginning to now.

Brett is looking at me like I've lost my mind. He's about to say something when the doctor and the nurse walk into the room. I stand up and head to the bed, opposite of him. Brett walks around and stands beside me. The doctor and the nurse check her over and remove the bandage from around her head. I can see glimpses of where they had to shave a portion of her beautiful hair. They then move the blankets back and raise up the gown she's wearing to take off the dressing she has on her side. The doctor nods his head at the nurse as she goes to a cabinet on the other side of the room.

"We are going to stop giving her the medication that's sedating her. We started weaning down the dosage last night. She won't wake up immediately. The medication is still in her system and will take hours to work its way out. In a few hours, we will turn the ventilator off and see how she breathes on her own. She may not fully wake for a couple of days. That's normal. Her body is healing, and sometimes rest is the best thing for it. I'll be back in four hours." He shakes our hands and leaves the room. The nurse gets new bandages on Kris and tells us to call if we need anything. I think she can feel the tension in the room. She gives us a small smile and leaves.

I don't know what to say. I don't want to fight with Brett. I sit back down and grab the remote. Flipping the TV on, I find an episode of Fast N' Loud to watch. Brett drops into one of the other chairs. I'm not going to tell him to leave, no matter how much it irritates me that he's here. I've never had an awkward moment with Brett, and I feel like I'm in uncharted territory.

Time drags by, and I try to keep myself busy. Brian drops by and seems surprised to see Brett waiting with me. He doesn't say anything, though. He's carrying my guitar and a bag, and hands it to me. It has some snacks and drinks inside. There's also a poker set. I glance up at him and he shrugs. "I figured we could play cards or something to pass the time. Have we heard anything?"

"They took her off the medication that's keeping her asleep. In a few hours, they're going to take her off the vent to see if she can breathe on her own. Then we just wait for her to wake up. We don't know how long that will take, though. It's all up to her."

He nods his head. I grab the poker set and set us up on the little table in the room. We gather round and get to playing. It's almost like old times. It makes the time fly by quicker, at least. Before I know it, the doctor and nurse come back in the room. We wait with bated breath when they turn the vent off. Her chest keeps rising and falling. "That's a very good sign, gentlemen. The medication is not repressing her breathing. I think she'll wake up sooner, rather than later. But we don't want to rush her. The closer she gets to waking up, the more she will start to move. We'll keep giving her small doses of pain medication to keep her comfortable. Just be patient. I know that's easier said than done. Talk to her, she can hear you. I see the guitar over there. You can play it, just don't get too loud and disturb the other patients." He gives us a nod and walks back out.

We sit back down and continue to play. Every few minutes, I glance over at Kristen to see if I can see any change. She looks better with the tube out of her mouth. She now has a tube across her face to give her oxygen.

After a few hours, Brian leaves. I know he has other things that he needs to do, but I appreciate him being here for support. I promise to let him know if there are any changes in her condition. I pick up the guitar and start to strum, and Brett starts to hum. Before I realize it, we're belting out some of our favorite songs. I'm glad that Kristen's room is at the end of the hall, away from most of the patients.

I start to play one of her favorite songs, Always, by Killswitch Engage. I start off and Brett joins in. Maybe it will reach her, make her come back to me faster.

I am with you always

From the darkness tonight to the morning

I am with you always

From the life until death takes me

Kristen

My eyes don't want to open. I feel like I'm floating in a fog, and I don't understand what's going on. I can hear music playing somewhere around me, and hear a deep voice singing. I know that voice, but I can't place it. I can make out a rhythmic beeping. I know that sound. I try to open my eyes, but they feel like they're weighted down. I try to lift my hand to my face, but it doesn't seem to want to cooperate. What the hell is going on? The beeping gets faster and the music stops. I can hear footsteps moving toward me and someone picks up each of my hands. I try to open my eyes again. Finally, I can see a sliver of light. It's so bright. I close my eyes again, as it feels like ice picks stabbing me. I say the only thing I can think of. "Derek." And I'm back in the fog.

Derek

I fall to my knees when she whispers my name. I keep hold of her hand and rest my forehead on the bed and cry. The relief is so great, I feel like my heart is going to explode. With that one word whispered from her lips, my world is righted. I feel her lightly squeeze my hand and I look back at her, but her eyes are closed again. I stand back up. "I'm here, baby. I'm not leaving you. I love you, Kris. Always."

I can finally breathe again. I say a silent prayer and thank the Lord for not taking her away from me. I see Brett lean down and kiss her on the forehead. He looks at me and gives me a sad smile. With one last squeeze of her hand, he walks out of the room. I sit and wait by her side until she opens her eyes again. I sing that song, over and over, hoping she'll wake up. Her eyelids flutter, then her hand twitches in mine. Pushing the call button, the nurse arrives and I inform her that Kris said my name and opened her eyes. She smiles, telling me that's a very good sign, and that it shouldn't be long before Kris is fully awake. I fall asleep sitting next to her, holding her hand.

I feel a hand running through my hair. It takes me a minute to realize what it is. I open my eyes and see Kristen looking at me, smiling. My world lights up with that smile.

Brett

With his name falling from her lips, my stomach drops. My heart hurts. I never knew I could hurt this bad. I thought when she left me, that was the worst pain. Or when she told me there wasn't a chance for us to be together. I was wrong. It was when she whispered another man's name, the man she wanted.

It may take some time, but I realize that they are good together. I'll have to learn to forgive Derek because we're brothers, no matter what. But I'll make damn sure he treats her right, something I always did before I broke her heart. I lean down and give her a kiss, silently tell her that I will always love her, and squeeze her hand. I look up and give Derek a small smile, then I walk out the door, leaving my heart in the room, shattered on the floor. Now it's time to move on.

I pass the nurse as she heads that way. "Leaving so soon? He said she woke up."

"She did. Just for a moment, and said his name." I see the look of pity on her face, and I wonder what she sees in mine. "I don't belong in that room with them. It's their time now."

She gives me a sad smile and continues to the room, while I head toward the elevators. I need some air. I need to clear my head and decide where I go from here. I text Brian, Jason, and Isaac to let them know she woke up. I figure that Derek is too wrapped up right now to think about it. Brian texts back that he wants me to come to the studio tomorrow. He thinks he has a project I may be interested in. Maybe it'll be the distraction I need, get me on the right track. I walk out into the parking lot and the sun is shining. It's going to be a great day.

EPILOGUE

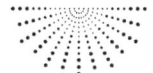

Kristen

It's been four months since the accident, and I was able to go back to work about a month later. I ended up staying in the hospital for a week. Since the accident, Derek has hardly left my side. The band has put off any tours for a while. They're going to work on a new album, so that will keep them at home. Derek asked me to move in with him, and of course I said yes. I don't want to spend a night away from him. I didn't want to stay in my apartment any longer. It didn't feel safe. Life has been pretty laid back for the two of us. Brett and Derek are on speaking terms, but they're not close anymore. Hopefully, with time, that will change.

I'm worried about Mallory. Apparently, Josh isn't who we thought he was and his daddy is a rich, vindictive bastard who wants her to pay for killing his son. We're still waiting to find out what is going to happen, but Jason hasn't left her side. We haven't seen hide nor hair of Stephanie, but I still keep my guard up. Derek changed his phone number again, so we haven't heard anything either. We still need to figure out what role she played in it all, or if it was just a coincidence. But I don't believe in coincidence.

I look over at Derek, standing at the sink. I can see the new tattoo that he has on his ribs. Always. He says it's because he was singing that song when I woke up. It's the way he feels about me, and the feeling is mutual. I will love him always, and I can't wait to see what the future holds for us. He glances over and sees me looking at him. He puts the glass down and walks toward me with a panty-melting grin on his face. It always amazes me how a man his size can move so gracefully. He makes his way to the couch, reaches down and grabs my hand, pulling me to my feet as he gazes into my eyes. "I love you, Kris." And with that, he kisses me. My life is perfect.

ACKNOWLEDGMENTS

My hubby and kids- Thank you for all the support, for forgiving me for spending so much time in my own little world, for having to eat so much take out because I was too busy to cook. I love y'all to the moon and back.

Cassandra – Thank you for being one of the best friends I ever could have asked for, for giving me a swift kick in the ass to write this book. If it hadn't been for you going with me to Nashville for my birthday, this dream of mine never would have been realized. Love you bunches!

Marie James – Thank you for being a mentor, for answering my million one questions and helping me through this crazy ride. I never would have gotten as far as I have without you help. And it all started when you met two crazy bitches in an airport.

My Betas – Darlene, Shawn, Jamie, Jaime – thank y'all for taking the time to help me get this book out there. Y'alls insight has been invaluable and very much appreciated. See y'all the next round.

ABOUT THE AUTHOR

Samantha Conley is a wife and mother who was born and raised in Texas. Her days are spent working in the medical field and her nights are spent with her family and writing her next book boyfriend. Just don't tell her husband. She has an addiction to watching the Food Network, rock music, Mexican food, chocolate tootsie roll pops, and Diet Dr. Pepper.

Make sure to stay up to date with all the upcoming releases by stalking her social media and newsletter (you won't get spammed, I promise!)
http://eepurl.com/cMbAqv

f facebook.com/authorsconley

BB bookbub.com/profile/samantha-conley

ALSO BY SAMANTHA CONLEY

Silver Tongued Devil Series

Down in Flames

Break Me Down

Down on My Knees

Crashing Down

Whiskey Bend Series

Pieces of a Broken Heart

(late May 2019)

Out of the Blue

(Fall 2019)

Printed in Great Britain
by Amazon

57566201R00139